A NEST OF
ONE'S OWN

A NEST OF ONE'S OWN

•

MARSHA DRISCOLL

AVALON BOOKS
THOMAS BOUREGY AND COMPANY, INC.
401 LAFAYETTE STREET
NEW YORK, NEW YORK 10003

PRINTED IN THE UNITED STATES OF AMERICA
ON ACID-FREE PAPER
BY HADDON CRAFTSMEN, BLOOMSBURG, PENNSYLVANIA

To my mother,
Mary Ennelle Hover Buckalew

She brought songbirds to our house

Chapter One

A sharp whistle broke into the sound of warblers and red-winged blackbirds. "Hector! Get back here right now! Come!" Paula Rosewood stretched up on her tiptoes to look toward the sound of the man's voice and the dog's answering bark. Across the open field of mown grass she could see the wire fence marking the boundary of Hadley Nature Preserve and the beginning of the plowed field beyond. A man in a red flannel shirt, jeans, and leather work boots slapped his hand against his thigh as an immense golden retriever bounded across the field toward him. Farther away, the white flash of a rabbit tail disappeared into the spring undergrowth, reprieved from the consequences of a chase by the energetic Hector.

That's a well-trained dog, to leave his quarry on command, Paula thought as she returned to her work. Approaching the wooden box nailed securely to a

1

pole about five feet from the ground, she peered through the small slit between the top of the box and the front panel. *Good, no wasp nest here,* she thought. Stepping to the side, she rapped a few times against the wood and watched to see what might come out of the hole in the middle of the front panel. Nothing moved. She grasped the small screw at the base of the panel, gave it a few turns, and lifted the entire panel up and out from the box.

The interior held a neat, square nest, snugly filling the bottom of the birdhouse, forming a miniature log cabin without a roof. "Hmph!" Paula snorted in disgust. She stuck her gloved fingers inside the nest, groping for eggs. The nest was empty of eggs or any sort of soft lining, and she gave a small, triumphant smile as she scraped the entire structure out of the box and onto the ground. *One down, twenty-four to go,* she said to herself.

Picking up her clipboard from the graveled track, Paula wrote "house wren—dummy nest—evacuated" in the space beside number one and moved closer to the fence where box number two stood. A tiny rusty-brown ball of feathers chirped angrily at her from a nearby ash tree, seriously aggrieved that anyone would touch his handiwork.

"Oh quit fussing," Paula chided him. "That's not a real home and you know it."

She repeated her ritual with the second birdhouse, found it empty, and recorded her find. As she turned back toward the track, she heard the dog barking behind her.

"Hey!" the man's voice called again. "What are you doing?"

Paula swiveled back to see him standing at the boundary fence staring at her belligerently. She stared back with equal venom. This had to be the

entrepreneur who had recently purchased this farmland, and who intended to turn the open fields into
an ethanol processing plant. The members of the
board for the nature preserve had attempted to purchase the land, but they had not been able to meet
the price offered by this man. Now Paula and the
other volunteers who had worked so hard to improve
this sanctuary visualized an industrial wasteland,
where before had been large, open cornfields.

At this close range Paula could see the man's rugged good looks. His light brown hair ruffled up in
the incessant Ohio wind, and his matching brown
eyes squinted against the glaring sun. He wasn't ex-
ceptionally tall, but he stood with an erect, almost
military posture that seemed to add to his height, and
his trim, muscular frame suggested a strenuous exercise regimen. His left hand rested on a fence post,
revealing a dull gold wedding band, and his right
hand caressed the head of the beautiful Hector. He
presented the picture of a man in absolute control of
himself and his surroundings.

"I'm doing my work," she called to him over her
shoulder as she once again turned back to the track
that led to the next set of birdhouses.

Numbers three and four sat in a sunny glade surrounded by a line of small pin oaks, and on top of
number four perched a compact bird with iridescent
blue feathers. He cocked his head as Paula approached, then took off directly away from her. As
she came closer to the nest, he pivoted and dove
sharply toward her, then pulled up and veered away
again. Paula blinked as the bird approached, then
laughed at him and kept moving until she reached
the birdhouse where she checked for wasps and
rapped on the side of the box.

Whoosh! A sudden fluttering, and out flew the female in a huff. Paula jerked back in surprise, even though she had half expected the bird to be there. With both parents diving fretfully, Paula quickly opened the house and checked the nest. On her tiptoes, she gently pulled the side of the nest and peered at the three perfectly white eggs there. Carefully closing the house, she recorded ''tree swallow nest— three eggs'' and moved to box number three. No signs of birds existed inside or outside of number three.

As Paula moved through the park checking the houses she felt a sense of hopefulness reassert itself. In spite of the changes to the neighboring land, she believed the Hadley Preserve would continue to provide an excellent sanctuary for a number of species. She had found two more swallow nests with three eggs each, and a bluebird nest with four sleeping fledglings. She had also cleaned out another wren's dummy nest that she had the good fortune to find before mamma wren decided she wanted that one.

At number twelve, Paula again checked for wasps and rapped on the side. This time, she congratulated herself for remembering to stand away from the hole, for a long black snake slithered rapidly out of the hole, falling the last few feet to the ground before disappearing in the thick grass.

''My gosh, does that happen often?'' a voice asked from the track.

Paula looked up and saw Hector and master standing quietly at the edge of the gravel path.

''Not too often,'' Paula remarked as she opened the box. The inside contained the remnants of another bluebird nest, with partial shells. She scraped the destroyed nest out and fastened the panel, then she recorded the destruction on her form. ''More often than I wish, but I suppose their cousins, the snakes, need to live, too. Actually, that was a black rat snake, or a pilot snake, and they're helpful in keeping the rodent population under control.'' She pulled a small can of grease from one of the deep pockets in her jacket and dabbed some around the base of the pole where it had apparently worn off.

She started to move past them toward the next clearing when the man stopped her by speaking. "I'm sorry if I startled you back there. I just wanted to make sure you weren't vandalizing the birds. I didn't see your clipboard, and I thought you were a kid tearing up bird nests for the heck of it."

Laughing at that, Paula showed him her records. "Hardly a kid, and I certainly wouldn't vandalize these nests. I seem to spend more weekends out here cleaning birdhouses than I spend cleaning my own house!" She felt a small pang of disloyalty, laughing with the enemy, but he seemed like a nice enough man.

"So why do you destroy the wren nests? I thought wrens were supposed to be wonderful little birds to have around." He started walking with her toward the next set of boxes.

"Oh, wrens are great; these house wrens can be a delight in the right place, especially in a garden where they will act as a natural pesticide. But they're an aggressive species that will take over an entire area and compete so fiercely that they endanger the other species. They will destroy other birds' eggs and fill up all the birdhouses with dummy nests. We aren't allowed to harm their eggs or a chosen nest, but we can evacuate dummy nests. That doesn't destroy the population, by any means, but it keeps them under control and gives the other species a chance to build."

As they approached the clearing, the man pulled

lightly on Hector's now attached leash and stayed back on the path. Paula quickly checked the houses and recorded two very young swallows. She thanked the man for keeping the dog away from the houses. "The birds tolerate the weekly check by humans, but I would hate to disturb them more than necessary."

"Of course," he said, patting Hector affectionately. "By the way, he doesn't bother you, does he?"

"Not at all. He's very well trained. Does he let strangers pet him?"

"He will be forever in your debt."

Laughing again, Paula held her hand palm down for Hector to sniff. Then she gently stroked his silky head and rubbed under his chin. "Hello, Hector. I'm Paula."

"He hasn't learned how to introduce me yet, but we're working on it. I'm Ned Andersen." He stuck out his hand and Paula shook it.

"Paula Rosewood. I volunteer for the Hadley Preserve. During nesting season we take a weekly count of the tree swallows and bluebirds. We've been trying to increase the population here by controlling the intruders and developing a friendly habitat." She looked sideways at him. "I suppose you were working, too, looking over the site of the new plant."

Her voice expressed some of her disapproval, and he chuckled softly. "Yeah, I guess you wouldn't be too happy with some concrete and steel monstrosity going up next door. I hope it doesn't hurt your ecosystem here too much."

Paula wondered at his tone. He sounded as if he were completely detached from the development, and as if any damage it caused would not be his responsibility. Maybe she had guessed wrong about his identity. "What were you doing?"

"I was just doing a preliminary survey of the place, thinking about pipelines and layouts. I have some responsibility for making sure the mess gets cleaned up properly." He glanced back toward the field but didn't elaborate any further.

Paula had checked five more birdhouses and they had nearly completed a circuit of the park. She pointed out a water snake sliding silently across a small pond just beyond the last clearing. "He's probably hoping to catch some of the young bull-frogs," she said just as they heard the unmistakable "plop" of one of the frogs leaving the side of the pond. "There comes dinner!" Ned and Hector waited patiently while she cleared a wasp nest from the last box and then walked back to the small parking area with her. "Thanks for giving Hector and me the guided tour, Paula," he said as Paula locked her clipboard in the base of the wooden box that held informational sheets for visitors to the preserve. "You obviously know this place well."

"There's a lot more to this area than just the meadow, you know." She pointed to the distant woods. "The woods take you to some great wetlands and a larger pond, and if you don't mind some hefty hiking, you can reach a secluded part of the Hadley Reservoir."

"I know. Actually, this is one of my favorite parts of the county, but I haven't been through the preserve for quite a while." He looked completely relaxed as he gazed out over the wild country.

"Is that the reason you're putting the plant here? Because it's your favorite part of the county? Don't you think that's a little self-defeating?"

He looked quizzically at her for a minute, judging the degree of anger in her tone. "I think you must have me confused with someone else. I really didn't have anything to do with the decision to put the ethanol plant in that field. My job is to make sure that we have adequate sewerage treatment for this section of the county, so that the water supply is properly treated and cleaned.'' He gave a crooked smile and added, ''I'm one of the good guys.''

Paula blushed a little and leaned down to pet Hector as a way to cover her embarrassment. ''Sorry. I guess I'm spoiling for a fight. I've been so frustrated about that land sale that I want to lash out at someone.''

Ned shook his head a little. ''I know how you feel, but I'm not the guy you have a quarrel with. Of course, as far as my job is concerned, this plant is less of a problem than a residential housing development would be, so I'm not as unhappy as you are.''

Paula sighed. ''I don't know which would be worse for the wildlife here. I just wish we had been able to purchase the land for the preserve.''

''Well, don't give up hope. There are other people who care about the environment, you know. Maybe things will turn out better than you expect.''

She gave him a cynical smile and opened her car door. ''Every cloud has a silver lining?''

''Or at least, somewhere, somebody can always use rain.''

''I just try never to go anywhere without my umbrella!'' She laughed.

''Surely you believe in the ultimate triumph of good over evil,'' he teased, but in a way that made her wonder if he might be more pessimistic than his previous words suggested.

''I believe we have to fight constantly against the negative consequences of greed.'' She spoke without any trace of humor.

Ned's eyes crinkled, but he managed to stifle the grin he felt pushing its way to his face. "I certainly hope that if we're ever in a fight, we're on the same side," he stated as Paula tugged open the rusting door of her ancient Escort.

She acknowledged the backhanded compliment with a lift of her head and a smirk. "Good-bye, Ned Andersen and Hector. It was nice meeting you both."

"Good-bye, Paula," Ned replied, and he pointed a finger at Hector, who barked twice in farewell.

Chapter Two

Entering his quiet house a few hours later, Ned smiled briefly in memory of Paula's anger. She reminded him somewhat of Annie in her willingness to take on a fight for the defenseless. He picked up a photograph of Annie that stood on the mantel over the large fireplace and stared at the much-loved face. "Hmm," he mused, "that girl even looks a little like Annie. Same red-gold hair, same freckles, same big blue eyes. She could be Annie's little sister." Of course Annie was about half a foot taller than that little bit of a thing who had stood on her tiptoes to check the bird nests.

He smiled again at the image and replaced Annie's picture. "Come on, Hector. We need to get something to eat before the big boys get here." He walked into the spotless kitchen, pulled out a package of ground meat and quickly formed two large hamburger patties. While the meat cooked, he made a salad, toasted a bun, and poured himself a large glass of milk. Then he placed one hamburger on his plate and one in Hector's dish along with a portion of dried dog food.

Ned kept up a steady stream of conversation with Hector as he read the daily newspaper and ate. "Look at this, boy. The court of appeals is allowing that development along Tucker Creek to go ahead. I thought the Supreme Court settled that last year, when they stopped development on the scenic river lands in Adams County. You just never know."

Hector, finished with his own meal, kept his eyes fixed on his master throughout the monologue. When he finished eating, Ned cleaned the kitchen with an efficiency that spoke of long practice and a natural preference for order. A short time later, he saw a dark green Land Rover pull into his wooded drive and two men get out of the car.

"Sean. Mark. It's good to see you again." Ned walked out to greet the men and shake their hands.

"How are you, Ned?" asked the taller of the two men. Sean Brady and his business manager, Mark Jackson, had known Ned for over six years. They had met him when Sean's company, Midwest Environmental Reclamation, or MER, had begun providing the technical equipment for the county's wastewater treatment facilities. At that time Ned had been acting as "circuit rider" for the smaller treatment facilities scattered throughout the county, and he had been impressed by Brady's commitment to combining high-tech waste recycling with land restoration programs. Mark Jackson represented the kind of employees Brady hired: dedicated, smart, and down to earth. He managed the Columbus-based firm while Brady scooted around the globe attending to several similar companies and a host of environmental crusades. For the past two years, though, Brady had spent considerably more time at home with his young wife.

"I'm doing fine, Sean," Ned replied. "How is Sarah holding up?"

"She's all right. This latest problem has her biting her nails, though. She never expected to spend the last three months of her pregnancy in bed. Only six weeks to go, though, and she has enough determination to handle anything for that long."

"I believe that. I don't know if I've ever met anyone with as much spunk as Sarah has."

"I'll second that," injected Mark, also shaking Ned's hand.

The men entered the house, and Ned brought out a set of maps of the southeast quadrant of the county marked with the various sewer systems of the townships and their connected outlying areas. They focused specifically on the area near the Hadley Reservoir and Nature Preserve. "The problem is that the area has been completely agricultural until now, and it is transforming into an industrial zone with no incorporated community close enough to assume the wastewater problem," Ned explained. "The county commissioners have agreed to let me determine the needs and assess whatever tapping fees are appropriate. The trouble is, I don't see how it is practical to bring that waste all the way into Centerville with our gravity-driven system. We'll have to use pumps of some sort, or build an entire facility for this one tiny area."

"Either way, it's going to cost the county some heavy capital," Mark responded.

"That's what I thought. I'd like you to look at these specs on the facility and give me some figures for at least those two options. If you can think of any alternatives, I'd appreciate hearing about them.''

"Let me see the septic tank use for residences in that quadrant, too. Maybe we can come up with a regional concept that your county commissioners would buy."

Sean rubbed Hector's head as he looked over the maps. "How did the county commissioners ever approve this plant? I thought the task force for preserving farmlands had mandated county-wide planning to limit unnecessary expansion of urban and suburban intrusion into farmland."

"Urged, not mandated. And the commissioners see this as an agricultural product-enhancement plant, not as an industrial facility. I'm sure the boost to the non-property tax base helped influence their decision."

"This borders on a small nature preserve, Ned. What's the environmental impact going to be?"

"ODNR says either they or Fish and Wildlife will do a study, but I would prefer for MER to do it with ODNR's review. I know that the advisory board for the preserve is pretty unhappy, and I met at least one volunteer out there this afternoon who looks like she might take a shotgun to the first construction worker she sees. I would prefer to have community support if we have to put out some big bucks, so I'd like to get that board on our side. The county commissioners are more environmentally aware than ever before, and we should take advantage of that."

The men spent nearly an hour more comparing residential, farm, and industrial sewerage needs for the Hadley area, and then another fifteen minutes listening to Sean describe the improvements to the nature preserve near Centerville, ten miles on the other side of Hadley.

"I'm proud of what the county has been able to do at Centerville, and I'd like the Hadley Preserve to develop the same way," Ned remarked. "I don't want this plant to disrupt what we've started here."

"Okay," said Mark. "We'll get on it." He rolled up the maps and other papers to carry to the car.

Sean stayed back with Ned for a few minutes. "Sarah gave me orders to ask you to come over to dinner Friday, Ned. She's going a little stir-crazy. She said you could come and cook supper for her, and that way we would all get a decent meal."

Ned smiled. "I would love to come. Tell her I'll be happy to cook if you do the dishes."

"It's a deal. I'll see you Friday."

Mark and Sean left, and Ned took Hector for his evening run down the country road along the river. Spring rains had swollen the water until it threatened to spill over onto the road in places. They followed the asphalt for nearly two miles and then returned along the same route, Hector's tongue lolling out by the time they ran up the steps to the cabin's porch. Man and dog collapsed to catch their breath and enjoy the evening call of the spring peepers.

"Whoever said the country is quiet never lived here," Ned quipped to Hector when they finally headed in for the night.

Once again Ned conducted his domestic chores with competence and chattered to Hector as he moved around the small, neat house. Finally he climbed into bed, put on a pair of reading glasses, and reached for a Robert Parker paperback. Hector lay down on the faded braided rug beside the bed, put his head on his paws, and closed his eyes.

For some reason, Ned found it difficult to concentrate on the mystery novel that night. He kept seeing the comical image of Paula Rosewood standing on her toes to count fledgling swallows. He remembered the fire in her eyes when she had glared at him across the fence, as if she dared him to threaten the well-being of the preserve. ''That's some little spitfire, Annie,'' he mumbled. ''I hope she learns to compromise, or she may get herself hurt out there.''

Giving up on the novel, he turned out the light and tried to sleep. After tossing and turning for another fifteen minutes, he finally admitted total defeat. ''Hector!'' The dog was standing immediately. ''Come on up.'' Ned sighed wearily. Happy to oblige, Hector jumped over Ned onto the bed and curled up contentedly against his master's back. After a few minutes, comforted by the heavy warmth on the other side of the bed, Ned finally drifted off himself.

Paula Rosewood had a few thoughts about Ned Andersen that night, too, but they weren't as complimentary as his about her.

''Honestly, Barb, he acted like he was the 'great protector of all outdoors.' *He* wanted to make sure that *I* didn't destroy any bird nests, and all the while he's deciding where to put the pipes to carry away the toxic waste from the plant.'' She sent an indignant snort over the telephone lines to her young, fellow biology teacher.

''Come on, Paula, you don't know that there are actually any toxic wastes from ethanol production.''

''No, but he said his responsibility was to clean up the mess.''

''At least someone takes that responsibility! It sounds to me like he got under your skin somehow. Maybe all this irritation doesn't have anything to do with his attitude toward the environment. How good-looking was he?''

''That has nothing to do with it,'' Paula protested, wondering even as she spoke if she were telling the truth. ''Just because they haul off their mess doesn't make it okay. Eventually it is going to be dumped somewhere. Eventually it remains a mess.''

''I'm going to have my own mess if I don't finish grading these papers for my classes. I'll be a little pile of toxic waste myself by the time my students get through with me.''

''Okay. Okay. I get the hint. I have plenty of my own work to do. I'm still trying to find a summer job, too. You haven't heard of anything, have you?''

''Personally, I'm giving a repeat performance of my 'hit show' Driver's Education. Take the word 'hit' literally.''

''Sorry. You may be a total masochist, but I'm not. I love teaching, but nothing short of a loaded gun will get me beside a sixteen-year-old driving a car for the first time.''

''Smart girl. Well, good luck. I'll see you tomorrow.''

Actually, Paula had completed all of her grading for the day. Unlike the loquacious Barb, Paula spent every minute of her planning period working. She usually arrived an hour early and left an hour or two late, but that way she kept most of her schoolwork at school. She hardly took time to sit down during the teaching part of her day, but neither did any other teacher she knew. After eight years of this job she felt she had mastered it enough not to spend three to four hours at night preparing, the way she did the first five years. Experience counted for a lot.

On the other hand, this past year she had spent a great many of her evenings working on a series of teaching texts with Sarah Wilson Brady. Sarah had received a grant to develop an interactive computer course for high school environmental studies, and Paula had acted as one of her paid consultants. The extra cash always came in handy, but more important, the work had revitalized Paula's teaching. In the same way that continuing education credits helped, any research or fieldwork always seemed to result in benefits for her students.

Paula had met Sarah in college when the two women had been paired up as lab partners in honors biology. At the time Sarah had been an extremely shy sixteen-year-old, whose anxiety nearly extinguished her brilliance. Paula, on the other hand, had been a bright, but not very serious, sorority pledge. Sarah stood nearly a full foot taller than Paula; she had dark, straight hair compared to Paula's short, wild reddish curls; and she never dated at all, while Paula had a different boyfriend every week. Interestingly though, they became very close friends for the next three years. Paula actually had an impressive intellect, and she didn't feel overwhelmed by Sarah's unusual intelligence. They worked well as lab partners and shared a number of other courses.

As the women matured, Paula's social life slowed considerably while Sarah blossomed after finishing her undergraduate work. They stayed in touch occasionally, but not with the same closeness they had as students. After Paula began teaching she rarely had time to do anything else except work on completing her M.S. in zoology. Then two years ago, Dr. Sarah Wilson had married Dr. Sean Brady, and the two of them had welcomed Paula into their world of environmental activism. By that time Paula had completed her master's degree and had reached the experience level in teaching that allowed her to have something of a personal life again; however, rather than resume the party-girl style of her youth, Paula found that she preferred quiet evenings with friends and their families.

Now Paula had completed the last revisions of her text for Sarah's program. Working with her old friend had been the best part of her life this past year, and Paula felt a little melancholy at the thought that the work was nearly finished. Glancing at the clock, she thought she would have time to call Sarah before bed. She knew that the last month of forced inactivity had made the normally energetic Sarah nervous and irritable, and she hoped, as the phone rang, that she was not disturbing a much-needed sleep.

"Sarah, it's Paula. Did I wake you?"

"Hi. No, I was waiting for Sean to get home. He had a business meeting tonight."

"Yuck. I just called to let you know I've finished the text."

"That's great! I can hardly wait to get it. Could you bring it over sometime this week?"

"Sure. I have to get out the last interim reports this week, but I could come on Friday. Would that work?"

"Perfect. Why don't you come for dinner? I'm going crazy by myself here all day. Poor Sean doesn't know who to worry about the most: me or the baby."

"Are you really okay?"

"Yep. No contractions at all for over a week. As long as I stay put and keep the tributaline pump going, I should be able to hold the baby in for the next six weeks."

"You're a marvel, Sarah. I'll bring you pickles and ice cream on Friday."

"Pickles only. Please. I can't stand anything sweet right now."

"Very dill pickles. I've got it. Maybe I can get a job as a waitress this summer."

"Oh, that reminds me. I have a line on a job you might be interested in. I need to check it out first, but I should have details by Friday."

"That's the best news I've had all day. Thanks."

Paula hung up the phone with a feeling of relief. If she could get some interesting work for the summer, not only would her finances be in better shape, but the time wouldn't hang so heavily on her hands. She loved helping out at the nature preserve, but it didn't really take up that much of her time, and for the past few years she had found herself almost dreading the summer vacation. Work had become her life.

She knew she needed to get out and start dating again, but she just couldn't bring herself to do it. During the school year she would tell herself that she did not have the time or energy to become involved with someone. No one would understand a teacher's time commitments for grading, attending meetings, chaperoning school functions, and on and on. Deep in her heart Paula knew this was simply an excuse, but she let herself use it. Then during the summer, she would tell herself that she shouldn't start up a romance that would only end in the fall: another excuse.

In her heart Paula knew that her real reason for not dating was her frustration with the many short-term relationships she had had. She no longer wanted the frantic social whirl of her youth; she wanted commitment and stability. But a long-lasting relationship seemed destined to remain only a wish. Instead, Paula kept herself busier than necessary during the school season, and loaded up with more classes than necessary during the summer. Last month her principal had rather dejectedly asked if she intended to complete a Ph.D., reminding her that most schools really couldn't afford to pay salaries at that level.

As she climbed into bed Paula had a flash of memory of the afternoon: Hector glowing in the sun as he raced happily across the field toward Ned Andersen. *Maybe I need a dog,* she thought.

Chapter Three

Ned drove slowly through the little town of Centerville on Friday evening. Since his promotion to director of the county department of water, he rarely got back to his old haunts. He had always liked Centerville, but his time as their water treatment specialist had been during the most difficult years of his life, and he didn't miss the memories this place aroused. Now he tried to enjoy the beauty of the town without thinking of the times he had speeded through here trying to get home to Annie.

Sean waited on the porch of their small home and held open the screen door for Hector.

"Where is she?" Ned asked.

"I'm in here, you slacker. Why don't you ever come to see me, Hector?" Sarah lay propped up on the sofa in the living room, cuddling Hector's head on her well-rounded middle.

"I brought you a peace offering, Sarah. Try to be nice." He handed her a jar of Claussen's dill pickles.

"You wonderful man! I will forgive you anything, even the fact that you have abandoned me in my hour of need."

"Come on, Sarah. I'm a boss, now. You know how it is with bosses. We're never around when you need us, and we're always around when you don't need us."

She and Sean laughed at this reminder of Sarah's own complaint about Sean at an earlier time. "Boss or not, I hear you agreed to do the cooking tonight."

"I guess that means I need to start the grill right away." Ned grimaced.

Sarah looked a little sheepish and explained, "It means you have to cook for four people instead of three."

"Is that because you're eating for two, or is someone else coming?"

"A friend of mine is going to be bringing some work she has done for my project."

"That's okay, Sarah. I think I can handle one extra burger."

"It's going to be more complicated than that, Ned. Sarah wants chicken." Sean laughed. "Come on out back and I'll help."

As they started the charcoal, Sean looked apologetically at his friend. "Sarah felt a little embarrassed about her friend coming over, Ned. She just asked her spontaneously, and then worried that you would think we were trying to matchmake. That isn't Sarah's style, and she didn't want you to get the wrong idea."

Ned laughed. "Don't worry about it, Sean. I still remember how to talk to women. And I know the two of you well enough to give you the benefit of the doubt." They talked about the Cleveland Indians' chances for a decent season and soon had the grill heating nicely.

Paula didn't pass through Centerville on her way to dinner. Instead, she left Preston High School half an hour later than she intended, stopped at the Big Bear Supermarket to get pickles, and sped through the country roads trying to reach Sarah's house at a decent hour. Her blouse clung to her back in the hot car, and she opened the window to try to cool off. *I don't care if I am in debt forever; the next car I buy will have air conditioning,* she promised herself.

Whipping into the Brady's driveway on the edge of town, she breathed a sigh of relief. When would she ever keep to her schedule? She had had plenty of time to get here, but she had been waylaid three times on her way out of the school building. Her clothes were wrinkled and damp from the hot drive, and her hair flew in every direction as the humidity frizzed her worse than a bad permanent; but she had at last arrived.

She banged on the screen door, calling Sarah's name.

"Come on in, Paula."

Paula found Sarah on the sofa and handed her the pickles.

"More Claussen's. I'm set for life!"

"How are you feeling, Sarah?" Paula asked, then jumped and screamed as a cold wet nose pressed against the back of her leg just below her hemline. She coiled around to see her assailant and let out a pleased exclamation. "Hector!" There couldn't possibly be two golden retrievers so large. Reaching down, she took the big reddish-brown head into her hands and smoothed the silky hair.

Sarah asked in surprise, "Do you two already know each other?"

"We're recent acquaintances. So, Hector, where is Ned Andersen? Or do you like to get out on your own sometimes?"

"We're usually a twosome, but sometimes he tries to slip away for a quiet little dinner with a lady friend. I've never known him to take on two women at once before, though."

The steady, deadpan voice from the kitchen door brought Paula back to her feet. "Hello, Ned Andersen."

"Hello, Paula Rosewood. I didn't think I'd see you again so soon." Ned's eyes sparkled with mischief. "Cleaned any houses lately?"

Paula suddenly remembered her crumpled blouse and windblown hair. With Sarah and Sean she never felt self-conscious about her after-school disarray, but standing in front of Ned's crisply ironed Dockers and polo shirt she felt like a frump. *A good offense is the best defense,* she thought.

"No, I haven't. Have you sold out to any toxic waste depositors lately?"

Behind Ned, Sean's eyebrows rose at least two inches, and Paula knew she must have sounded petulant. "Sorry, Hector," she said, looking away from Ned and back to the dog. "I didn't mean to insult you. I know you wouldn't associate with anybody but the 'good guys.' "

Ned seemed willing to ignore Paula's discomfort completely. "Actually, I'm here to see who wants toxic waste put on their chicken. Sean swears that this barbecue sauce will not kill you, but I personally won't be responsible if anyone eating it is consumed by spontaneous combustion."

Everyone but Sarah declared themselves willing

to take the risk, and she blamed her condition rather than the sauce. Sean settled her on a chaise on the back patio while Paula and Ned finished gathering food from the refrigerator. Hector guarded the grill like the gentleman he was, only gulping down a piece of chicken when Paula surreptitiously held a portion of her own under the table for him. Ned watched her pretense of wide-eyed innocence, knowing full well that she was attempting to subvert his dog, and enjoying the idea that she thought she could fool him.

When everyone had eaten their fill, Ned called Hector for a walk and they roamed through the wooded lot behind the house. Sean kept his promise of washing the dishes, leaving Paula to keep Sarah company.

"Paula, I hope I didn't make a mistake asking you and Ned here at the same time. I didn't know you had met, and to tell you the truth, I didn't really think about it. I just wanted the company of my friends."

"I'm the one who should apologize, Sarah. I just felt so defensive. There he stood, looking so beautiful and clean—and there I stood, a total mess. I think he's too neat, or something. I want to throw dirt on his shoes."

Sarah laughed. "Please don't. If you take this job I'm going to tell you about, you may have to work with him. He's pretty easygoing most of the time, but I don't know how he would handle someone deliberately getting him dirty."

"What job?" Paula focused immediately on the most important point.

"I think you will really like this. You know that MER always does a study of the natural ecology of a site before they help build a plant. Usually Sean does these himself, just because that's the work he likes to do. But he has had so many other obligations this year that I was planning on taking over that work this summer.''

''You aren't in any shape to do that now, are you?''

''I can hardly get up long enough to go to the bathroom. But that's okay. My misfortune is your good fortune. It looks like the county is going to put in a mini-treatment site over near the Hadley Reservoir because of the new ethanol plant. That means doing a study of the area to help keep the ecosystem as healthy as possible. You can do the study and work with Ned and MER to protect that land bordering the preserve.''

Paula's mouth fell open. ''I don't know whether to jump up and down with joy or shoot you. Isn't this sort of like sleeping with the enemy, Sarah?''

Sarah shrugged her shoulders. ''Look, Paula, the world isn't a perfect place. When I first met Sean I thought he was a starry-eyed idealist trying to do the impossible. Now you think that what MER does isn't good because it isn't idealistic enough. All I know is that we have to do what we can. You aren't going to stop that plant now; the county commissioners clearly want it. But you have a chance to help see that the environmental impact is minimal or even beneficial.''

''I know you're right. I tell my students this all the time. We have to be realistic, and we have to work for what we think is right.'' She looked through the gathering dusk at Ned throwing a stick into the woods for Hector to retrieve. ''Where's his wife?''

''What?''

''Ned's wife, what's the story? He wears a ring.

Doesn't he take her with him when he goes to visit friends?''

''Annie's dead.''

Paula turned and stared at Sarah, horrified at her own tactlessness. ''I'm really sorry, Sarah. Was she a friend of yours, too?''

''I never met her. She died two years before I came here, about five years ago. Sean knew her.''

''What happened?''

''She had ovarian cancer. Ned was totally devoted to her. I think maybe he still is.''

Watching the crisp teamwork between Ned and Hector, Paula wondered if perhaps Ned had transferred his devotion to the animal, but she thought better of saying so. ''He seems like a nice enough man.''

''Sean and I like him a lot. Do you think you want this job?''

''Quite honestly, it sounds perfect. I can't think of any better way to spend my summer than out in the field studying the things I love.''

Sarah smiled knowingly. ''Great!''

The door opened and Sean stepped out of the kitchen just in time to hear Sarah's remark. ''Does that mean she'll take it?'' he asked, kissing his wife on the top of her head.

Paula answered for herself. ''I would be thrilled. When do I start?''

He explained the protocol and assured her that Mark Jackson would have everything she needed to conduct her work. ''At this point there have been a number of hitches slowing down the plant construction, and that is good. You can start as soon as the school year ends. We'd like a preliminary overview in two weeks and an initial report in six weeks. You'll need to continue with some of the evaluation throughout the year and into next year's breeding season.''

Ned had returned from the woods, and Hector immediately flopped on top of Paula's feet. She absentmindedly reached down and scratched behind his ears. Ned watched her without interrupting the conversation, guessing what it involved, and wondering if she would be able to compromise enough to see the job through.

''I don't know how I'll be able to keep my mind on teaching for the rest of the year. It's a good thing we only have three weeks left.'' Paula sighed.

As the party ended, Paula leaned down and hugged Sarah hard. ''Take care of yourself. And thank you. I really needed something like this.''

''I know what that's like, remember? And I'll be happier knowing I trust the person doing the job.''

Paula and Ned walked to their cars together, and Ned held her door open for her. As she sat behind the wheel, he looked in at her feet.

''Yep. You really do reach all the way to the gas pedal. I wondered about that.''

Paula stuck her tongue out and made a face at him. ''No short-people jokes allowed.''

''I was just worried about your safety.''

''Right.''

Hector ended the bantering by thrusting his head into Paula's lap for one more scratch.

''Hector!'' Ned scolded him. ''You're being boorish. I'm sorry, Paula. He usually behaves better than this.'' He raised an eyebrow at her. ''I can't imagine where he got the idea that he could get away with this.''

''Please don't scold him.'' Paula admitted, ''I was asking for it and he knew it. I love dogs, and he's the best.''

"If you appreciate him that much, I can't scold him." Ned smiled at the compliment and waved good night. As he drove back to his own home far out in the county, Ned kept seeing Paula with Hector lying on her feet. Her eyes had sparkled with excitement about the new job, and the dying light had cast a halo of glints around her hair. Hector had lain on her feet the way he used to do with Annie when he was a puppy. Suddenly the similarity between that image and memories of Annie was so strong he felt as if he had been sucker punched. He pulled over to the side of the road, waiting for the old familiar pain to recede. "Oh, Annie, girl. What am I going to do?" he whispered when he finally started down the road again.

No second thoughts bothered Paula as she zoomed back toward Preston. "Thank you, thank you, thank you!" she shouted out the window. The job certainly answered her prayers, and she could hardly wait to begin.

Chapter Four

In spite of anticipating the new job, time did not hang heavily for Paula over the next three weeks. Pushing to fill every minute of instruction time with her students, Paula loaded her own time with grading labs, quizzes, and extra-credit reports. As usual, a handful of seniors teetered dangerously on the edge of failing her elective environmental science course, and as usual, she let them work their way out of their own problem by doing extra work. Of course, it meant that she had extra work, too, since it required her to grade the papers. No matter how lenient she might be in granting another chance, ultimately the student had to produce quality work or not pass. She hated the few times someone ended up in summer school in order to graduate, but she would not compromise her standards. She was considered a very strict teacher, yet her elective course remained one of the most popular in the school.

Eventually the final grades were submitted and the last yearly reports completed. Paula locked her equipment cabinets and turned in all of her keys. Much to Principal Reinhardt's gratification, she informed him that she would not be working toward her Ph.D. this summer, and she waved a gleeful farewell as she left the classroom behind for nine weeks.

Armed with a notebook produced by Sean, Paula began early the next morning in her survey of the field adjacent to the preserve. Following her own instincts as well as Sean's suggestion, she began with an overview of the area. Several hours later she returned to her car, hot, thirsty, and covered with ticks. She knocked them off her jeans, glad that she had had the foresight to wear long pants and high boots. Her head, covered with a scarf, escaped the infestation, but she longed to return home and spend some serious time under a hot shower.

As she reversed the car out of the field, she listened to an emergency weather report on the radio, learning that a tornado watch had been called for the late afternoon all across the county. Paula looked at the sky, noticing the beginning of dark clouds to the southwest. She would be very glad to reach home.

Suddenly she thought of Sarah Brady. Yesterday Paula had spoken with Sean about the study and he had mentioned commuting to Chicago today. Poor Sarah must be miserable all alone in that house and unable even to get up. Putting her own discomfort behind her, Paula steered toward Centerville rather than Preston. Already the wind had begun to pick up speed and ferocity, and by the time Paula arrived at Sarah's house, the rain had begun.

"Sarah, are you in here?" she called through the door.

"Paula? Come on in. I'm upstairs."

Paula shut the wooden door as well as the screen and mounted the steps to the bedroom. "How are you doing?" she asked as she entered the room.

Sarah rested on a large bed with books and papers piled all around her. A large pitcher and glass stood on the bedside table, and a wheeled cart full of pickles, bread, peanut butter, and fruit lay within easy reach.

"My gosh. You could survive forever with that stash!"

"Sean's big on being prepared."

"Well, it's a good thing, since you're here all alone and you aren't supposed to get up."

"What are you doing here? I thought you started your survey today."

"I did. Can't you smell the great outdoors on me?"

"Is that what it is? I wondered." They both laughed.

"Actually, I was on my way home to a much-needed shower when I heard the weather report. There's a tornado watch in effect, and I thought you might like some company."

"Paula, you're an angel." Sarah smiled. "Why don't you go take a shower? There's no lightning yet, and it may be your last chance for a while."

Paula had extra clothes in the trunk of her car and ran out to get them. By the time she returned, she was drenched and battered by hailstones. She cleaned up and then turned on the radio to listen for the weather report again. The howling wind had become frightening, and Paula suggested that she help Sarah move downstairs.

Just then the telephone rang, and Sarah spent the next few minutes reassuring her mother that she was not alone in the face of bad weather. Finally the two women began making their way carefully down the steps to the rec room on the lower level, where they once again propped up Sarah's feet. Halfway down the stairs, the phone began ringing again, but they couldn't stop to answer it until Sarah was settled. By then the caller had hung up.

Paula gathered flashlights and the radio just as the local tornado siren began sounding. She stuck her head out the front door but couldn't see anything worse than clouds and rain.

"The weather report says they have spotted a funnel cloud to the northeast of us," Sarah exclaimed. "The worst must be past us."

"Good," sighed Paula. "I hate tornado season. It's the worst part about living here."

The telephone started ringing again, and Paula raced up stairs to answer it.

"Who is this? Where's Sarah?"

She laughed into the speaker. "Relax, Sean. This is Paula. Sarah's downstairs because we had a tornado warning." She carried the phone to Sarah and listened to her reassure one more person that she had company during the weather crisis.

"They'll be here in a few minutes, Paula," Sarah informed her. "Ned met Sean at the airport and is bringing him home."

By the time Sean and Ned arrived the weather seemed to have cleared enough for everyone to relax, but Ned suggested that he follow Paula home just to be safe.

"What exactly do you think you might do to protect me from a tornado, Ned? It's not likely to answer your call as obediently as Hector," Paula quipped.

"No, but I do have a phone in my car and I could

call someone if you got carried into the next county,'' he replied.

Why does this man irritate me so much? she wondered. She kept wanting to rattle him, to make him lose that sense of absolute control. ''His hair looks too neat,'' she thought nastily to herself, but aloud she said, ''If you're going to follow me, let's get going. I probably left all my windows open this morning.''

She sped along the back roads to Preston, hoping Ned might have difficulty keeping up with her, but when she pulled into the small parking lot of her apartment building, he and Hector turned in right behind her. The rain and hail had started up again, and she asked him if he wanted to come in and wait for things to clear up.

Ned made a little grimace and replied, ''I'm not sure things are going to clear up that easily.''

The double meaning of his words struck Paula, but she let them pass and simply thanked him for his concern. Then she raced for her building, and he left. She had, in fact, left two windows wide open and she had a mess to clean up. By the time she had mopped up the water and picked up the over-turned plants from her windowsill, she noticed that the storm had built in intensity again. Paula shut the windows and turned on her television to check the radar report. Another major storm followed the ear-lier one, and now seemed headed directly toward Preston.

Paula knew that she overreacted to tornado warn-ings sometimes, and she refused to let her neighbors ridicule her by running to the basement this time. She did decide to retrieve her flashlight, though, and she pulled a chair over to the closet to enable her to reach the high shelf. Just as she stood on her tiptoes to stretch for the flashlight, she heard the warning siren begin, and the next thing she knew, a large train drove through her apartment at two hundred miles per hour.

Paula was knocked off the chair by the force of the winds as the roof of the apartment building flew into a thousand pieces. She had a few seconds of absolute terror before she hit her head, landing in a heap inside the closet and pulling several coats down on top of her. This probably saved her from more serious damage because her front windows shattered, sending glass and debris throughout the apartment. The storm raged, destroyed, and passed on while Paula lay semiconscious in the shambles of her building.

Eventually the funnel cloud lifted, and the forces driving the vicious whirlwind loosened their grip on the air. Paula stirred under the heap of clothing, vaguely aware that she hurt, but not conscious enough even to localize the pain. Drifting in and out of consciousness, she knew only that she wanted to hide, that she felt frightened. Tinnitus assailed her ears, but through the ringing she heard a series of sharp detonations. Each explosion pierced her head and forced her to withdraw even farther under the pile of coats.

Something pushed against her back and she felt more explosions in her ears. "Stop it! Stop it!" she tried to scream, but her voice came out as a whisper.

The explosions did stop but were replaced by a whining, whimpering buzz and a renewal of the pushing against her back.

"Paula! Can you hear me?" Now a voice separated from the medley of sounds in her head. "Paula!" She heard the voice coming closer, but she only wanted to retreat, not answer the call. One more sharp explosion, this time practically inside her head.

"Paula! Good boy, Hector. Paula, can you hear me?" She felt a weight being lifted from her, and she tried to crawl farther back under the coats. "Paula? It's okay. It's Ned. Don't try to move, Paula. Everything is going to be okay."

She heard Ned's soothing voice drone on softly as if he were comforting a baby, and she thought of Sarah's baby and hoped it was all right. Did Ned have a baby? Why was he talking so softly? She felt the cool air as he lifted the last of the debris from her and pulled off the coats. She tried to focus on his face, but suddenly Hector's cold nose pressed against her cheek, and she felt a warm, wet tongue licking her nose.

Out of the confusion of sensations only that one fact registered in her consciousness. "Yuck! Hector, you're giving me a dog kiss! Go away!"

Ned started laughing and pulled Hector back out of the closet. "Come on, Hector. Leave her alone. She must be all right if she can get mad at her rescuer!"

Paula saw Ned leaning over her in the closet, and she tried to sit up. A wave of nausea swept through her and the next thing she knew she was halfway in Ned's lap with her head cradled in his arm.

"Paula, don't try to sit up yet. You hit your head pretty hard, and you've probably got a concussion. The squad is downstairs helping some of your neighbors, but someone will be up in just a minute."

She relaxed, not willing to make herself sick again and not all that uncomfortable right where she was. She knew she couldn't think clearly, and Ned's strong arm felt warm and reassuring. She closed her eyes, and the next time she opened them she was being placed in the back of an emergency rescue vehicle. Ned stood beside her and patted her hand.

"Paula? Are you back with us? They're taking you to the emergency clinic. Don't worry, I'll be right behind you."

Paula tried to nod but only made her head hurt more. She shut her eyes again, not losing consciousness, but maintaining only a dim awareness of the ride to the clinic. By the time the medics had her out of the ambulance, Ned stood by her side again. Her stayed with her for the next two hours as she had X rays taken, tiny lights flashed in her eyes, and medical fingers pushed into her spleen and liver. With each passing minute her thoughts cleared more, but her headache grew worse.

Finally the physician allowed her to sit carefully on the side of the examining table while he spoke quietly to Ned. The doctor left and Ned walked back to Paula's side with a sympathetic look on his face.

"How terrible do you feel?" he asked.

"Probably only twice as bad as I look."

He laughed. "You must feel pretty miserable, then."

Paula snorted, "Well, even you got your hair messed up, so I'm not going to get all defensive this time."

"Come on, Miss Smart Alec. The doctor says they don't have enough beds available for goldbricks like you. You can come home with me, since I'm a trained paramedic. There's not much left of the night, and there's nothing left of your apartment, so you might as well come and let Hector take care of you."

If she had felt better, Paula might have protested and gone to a motel, but she couldn't tolerate the thought of going somewhere alone just then. In fact, she could hardly think at all, so traumatized did she feel. By the time they reached Ned's house, she just wanted a place to collapse. He offered her the bedroom, but she retained enough logic to point out that she could sleep on the sofa with a foot of spare room, while he would have trouble fitting at all. Ned accepted her argument and soon had her covered and comfortable.

As he climbed into his own bed, Ned realized that Hector had stayed downstairs with Paula. That dog had certainly attached himself quickly to that little girl. He caught himself, suddenly aware that he did Paula a great injustice by equating her tiny size to immaturity. She was nearly thirty years old, only half a dozen years younger than he, and she wouldn't appreciate being patronized. But she certainly had looked young and helpless, lying pale and frightened in the remains of her closet. Ned felt a protective lurch of his heart, a desire to protect Paula followed by the rapid need to protect himself. Staring up at his ceiling, Ned carefully replaced the chinks that had developed in his emotional armor as he watched Paula bravely ignoring the loss of her home.

A few hours later, he awoke to Hector blowing hot breath on his face and pawing insistently at the mattress. "What is it boy? Do you need to go out?" Hector whined in response and moved to the bedroom door.

Following the retriever to the floor below, Ned saw Paula sitting up on the sofa wrapped in a light sheet, shaking with tiny spasms as if shivering with cold. The warm June night air flowed gently through the open window, all traces of the earlier violent weather completely vanished. Ned spoke softly, not wanting to frighten Paula more. "Hey there, Paula girl. Are you all right?"

She didn't respond at all but continued to sit there shaking. Alarmed, Ned crouched on the floor in front of her and grasped her hands in his. They felt icy, and he rubbed them gently to warm them. "Paula?"

She stared ahead, not seeing him at all, and he realized she wasn't even truly awake but was caught in that trancelike place reserved for trauma victims. He sat up beside her on the couch, and keeping her two hands in one of his, put his other arm around her shoulders. Gently he rocked her back and forth and spoke in that same soft tone he had used when he found her. "It's all right, Paula. Everything is going to be all right. Just relax. You're safe now."

Over and over he repeated the words, gradually changing his tone from one of quiet soothing to one of matter-of-fact comfort. As he speeded up his words, he rubbed her hands and arm briskly and increased his volume. "Paula! Wake up now. Come on and wake up. That's a girl."

Paula blinked her eyes a few times, took a deep breath, and suddenly looked at Ned with an expression of total confusion. "What happened? I feel very strange. Was I having a nightmare?"

"Don't worry about it. You were reacting to all the shock. I should have expected it, but you seemed so calm and collected earlier that I assumed you weren't bothered by things like having your house blown apart."

An onslaught of emotions suddenly burst through the protective barrier of her shock and Paula wanted to scream at this man who could make a joke at the devastation she had just experienced. Overwhelming rage surged through her whole body, and she raised a hand to strike him. Fortunately he expected it and reached for her hand just before she connected with his face. With a shock she realized what she had tried to do, and she suddenly burst into tears of humiliation, impotence, and grief. Ned put both arms around her then and let her sob until she had exhausted herself..

By the time her crying finally stopped, Ned's shirt was drenched and Hector had worked himself into a frenzy of distress for her. Paula hiccupped a few times and then started to giggle when she looked at Ned. His shirt was a disaster from her tears, his hair, touseled from sleep, fell into his eyes, which were dark and strained from fatigue, and his cheeks bore the rough signs of a needed shave.

"Are you laughing at me, Ms. Rosewood?"

"I'm just very happy to see that you are a member of the human race after all. I had begun to think you were some kind of alien who never got messy."

"My mother always insisted on good personal hygiene," he retorted with feigned injured dignity. "Would you like a cup of coffee? My mother also taught me manners."

Predawn gray light filtered through the windows, and Paula knew neither of them was likely to get more sleep after her hysterics, so she gladly accepted the offer. She started to get up to help, but Ned waved her back down.

"You may still have a little vertigo. Just stay there and reassure Hector."

He bustled around in the kitchen, then made a quick trip upstairs to change shirts and restore the reputation of his personal hygiene. In a short time he reappeared with a tray of coffee, toast, and strawberries. Paula thought she had never tasted anything so wonderful.

Ned sat opposite her in an easy chair, sipping on

his own coffee while Paula gratefully swallowed the hot, welcome drink. "Thank you, Ned. You're very . . . kind."

He looked questioningly at her. "You sound surprised."

Paula shook her head. "No. I started to say 'efficient,' but that didn't seem fair. You are efficient, but I think maybe 'kind' is more accurate."

He scrutinized his coffee cup as if searching for some treasure in its depths. "Sometimes efficiency helps kindness be more effective." He emphasized the word "sometimes," and Paula wondered about the times his efficiency wouldn't have helped his wife.

"Speaking of efficiency," he continued in a lighter tone, "I suggest that you let me help you out with transportation today. If you want to go check out the plant site for damage, we could stop there first. I need to get to my office sometime this morning, but just for a short while to check on a few things. Then we could head back in and see what's left of your apartment."

"That's a lot for you to do for me, Ned. Maybe you should just take me back so I can get my car."

He grimaced slightly and sighed. "Two problems with that. One, you shouldn't be driving yet. And two, you haven't seen your car yet."

Paula shut her eyes and put her hand up to her forehead. "Please don't tell me a tree fell on my car last night."

"Nope."

"Thank goodness."

"The roof blew onto it."

Paula's head sank to her knees and she covered her head with both hands. Ned watched her as her shoulders began shaking and he feared another serious cry. "Paula?"

The shaking continued and Paula began to emit little gasps. Ned became truly fearful until suddenly he realized she was convulsed with laughter. "Paula? Are you all right?"

"Oh, quit asking me that. I'm not going to crack up." She sounded irritated, but she spoiled the effect by starting to giggle again. Tears squeezed out of the corners of her eyes and she began to hold her stomach as her laughter became contagious, and Ned began to chuckle, too. Each time Paula brought her giggles back under control, she would look at Ned sitting there in his crisp, clean clothes telling her that her roof had fallen on her car. Then she would feel a bubble starting up from her diaphragm, and suddenly she would be clutching her ribs and laughing again. Ned's own laughter increased each time she started up again. Hector ran from one to the other, barking continuously and adding to the general hilarity. Finally she rose from the sofa and walked to the kitchen to get completely away from both of them and bring herself under control.

Ned left her alone until he thought it might be safe to approach her. He found her standing at the kitchen sink looking out across the wooded lot at the rising sun. Her face shone with a peace that belied all the chaos of the previous night, and she smiled when she turned toward him.

"My entire life may have caved in, Ned Andersen, but at least now I'm going to get a car with air conditioning."

"Every cloud has a silver lining?" he asked.

"Not necessarily. But at least somewhere, somebody always needs rain."

Chapter Five

Paula maintained her positive attitude throughout the remainder of the morning. The preserve and the adjacent site escaped the most devastating wind, and only a few lost branches marred the glorious beauty of the place.

"This won't hurt anything. It's just nature's way of pruning the trees," Paula remarked as she examined one of the larger limbs. "All of these were dead, anyway, and they don't seem to have ripped off live wood." Then she noticed that several of the larger limbs had woodpecker-drilled holes in them and she inspected them more carefully. Three separate wren nests had been destroyed along with their contents. She couldn't determine if the fledglings had still been in the nests, since a predator might well have already cleared them out.

She felt a wave of compassion for the feisty little birds, but she stifled it quickly. "It's no big loss,"

43

she thought, "as long as the bluebirds and swallows didn't lose any chicks." With a shake of her head she pushed the thought of the wrens out of her mind.

She moved back through the field and down an incline. Across the fence she could see the nesting boxes in the preserve, and she began watching the feeding dives of the swallows rather than her own feet. Within seconds she found herself ankle-deep in mud.

Standing at the top of the slope, Ned grinned at her. "Hey! You didn't get your feet wet, did you?"

"Thanks for the sympathy," she mumbled as she felt the sucking mud pull at her boots. She wondered why the mud was so much worse here, and realized she was standing in the middle of a natural pond. The heavy rains had filled the basin, and the deeper area still held about a foot of water. The rest of the land was draining rapidly, leaving the deep, sticky mud.

Undaunted by the messiness, Paula followed the contours of the field, noticing how the bottomland had been built up in places to create effective drainage. The farmer's technique effectively dried out the entire basin, leaving him with perhaps three acres of field that would otherwise have been swamp. Paula admired his ingenuity at the same time that she regretted the lost wetland.

Finally becoming tired of carrying the extra pounds of mud, Paula trudged back uphill to Ned. Her eyes sparkled with enthusiasm as she described the possibilities for restoring the area to its natural condition. "If we simply reversed the drainage effects, the area would completely restore itself within a couple of years!"

He nodded approval, and Paula could see him thinking. "I think we might be able to work something into the water treatment plant that would help out. Have you seen what we have at Centerville, or what they've done on the coast of Lake Erie by Sandusky?''

''I've been to both places, but I have to admit I spent more time studying the flora than the engineering.''

''Well, it's time to broaden your education. Let's go to my office, and I'll get you some information.''

By the time they arrived at the Preston County Water Treatment Facility, Paula's legs felt like they were encased in cement. The cool, clear morning already showed signs of dissolving into another muggy, storm-laden afternoon. Watching the beginnings of clouds collecting on the western horizon, Paula felt a small shudder run down her spine. She resolutely turned her back on the clouds and looked around the impressive facility.

''Have you ever been here?'' Ned asked.

''When I first started teaching I used to bring my environmental science class here every spring. Then four years ago, the school district started having such financial trouble that they canceled all field trips. Since then I've tried to encourage my students to come out here on their own to see the place, but I haven't been back for several years.''

''So you're the one responsible for that. Every year we get at least one carload of kids out here. They say their teacher told them to come. They're always pretty skeptical until somebody gives them a tour of the place, and then they usually become converts.''

''I'm glad to know they really come. I hear reports, but I've learned to take their statements with the grain of salt I reserve for brownnosing.''

''A wise teacher.'' Ned smiled, remembering his

own high school attitude. "If you haven't been here for a while, you should look around. We've added some interesting improvements in the past three years. I'll only need to be here for a little while."

Just then a young woman wearing jean shorts and a T-shirt came storming out of the small building labeled "office." "Ned, the whole system in the northeast quadrant is off-line! We lost power there last night, and something is wrong with the backup generators. I think there's a computer glich, because we thought the backups had kicked in until I went out there this morning. Nothing has turned over for about six hours and if we don't get that sludge stirring soon, we'll be a week getting the machinery working again."

Ned ran a hand through his hair, and Paula marveled at how it immediately fell perfectly back into place. Even in a time of crisis, he always looked perfect. *It must be a curse,* she thought. *Any man who can always look that good must be hated by every woman he knows.*

In spite of his unruffled looks, Ned obviously worried about the problems with his system, and Paula waved him away to his work. "I'll be looking around out here," she assured him. She wandered over the grassy field to the moat surrounding the facility.

Two years ago some of Paula's students had returned to school with a description of the moat. The waterway flowed gently around the entire park and into the river, providing a barrier as effective as a high fence or wall, but adding much more to the beauty of the place. Mallards and Canadian geese serenely floated by or wandered along the grassy shore of the moat, giving the entire facility the flavor of a park rather than a treatment facility. In fact,

Paula realized, the plant looked totally different from how it had appeared when she last visited here four years ago. Ned's tenure as director began three years ago, and already he had made major changes in this facility.

Large, open tanks churned steadily, speeding the natural aeration process to clean the water. Biological waste would eventually cleanse itself from the water supply even without these treatment plants, but the usage rates were so high that concentrated populations could not afford to wait for nature. Therefore, the treatment plant speeded up nature's process by concentrating the organic content, rapidly turning the water, and then removing the sludge.

Paula walked past the second set of tanks, the ones in which the sludge was skimmed off and sent to another area to be dehydrated even further. If these machines stopped as the ones in the northeast had, they would clog up quickly, and the slightly musky odor would rapidly become very nasty. Not only would he have a mess to clean up, but Ned would also start receiving complaints from the neighbors.

On the far side of the tanks stood a new building. Its position suggested that it might house the final processes of filtering the remaining waste and adding a chlorine product to kill bacteria. Paula entered and saw a young man hosing down a set of steps leading to an iron catwalk.

"May I help you, ma'am?"

"I'm just looking around while I wait for Ned. Is this a filter room?"

"No ma'am. That's the building right behind you."

"Oh. What's in here?"

He grinned with pride. "This is the new UV treatment room. Come on up and take a look."

Paula looked down at her mud-caked boots and held one up for his inspection.

"Oh, don't mind that. I'll be cleaning out mud all day today."

Up on the catwalk she watched crystal clear water flowing through narrow troughs in which long panels of pale violet lights shone eerily. "What is this for?"

Setting the hose back on its hook, he jumped up beside her. "Those are ultraviolet lights. They kill the bacteria, like sunshine would in the natural process, but we increase the concentration in these troughs."

Paula asked, "Do you still have to add the chloride?"

"Not anymore." Ned answered her from the doorway. "We only used it in the summer, anyway, when people are likely to be swimming or wading in the river. Chlorination has some potential carcinogenic properties, so it was always a trade-off. Which was worse: serious bacterial infections or possible cancer?"

The younger man jerked his thumb in Ned's direction, "When Ned learned about this UV set-up, he campaigned with the county commissioners until he got it. Now we don't have to make that trade. We can kill the bacteria and not put anything extra into the water."

Paula thought about the impact of Annie's cancer and wondered if Ned ever blamed himself for her illness. The best treatment for killing bacteria had been chlorination, and the horrendous devastation of typhoid and dysentery could kill many more people than were likely to develop cancer. But it must have galled him to know that his work for the good of the community might have had any connection to her illness. Paula shoved the thoughts away and turned to her guide.

"Thanks for letting me come up. I hope I didn't track too much mud."

"Don't worry about it, ma'am. Hey, boss, did you hear about the generators up in . . ."

"I heard, I heard. About five times now, Joe. How's everything here?"

"We're in good shape."

"Good. I want you to go northeast with Karen and get those generators back on-line. I'm going to be out, but I've got my pager with me. Let me know if you're having problems."

"Sure thing. See you later." Joe jumped easily back down from the catwalk, and Paula felt even older than she had when he had called her "ma'am."

"I found some papers on combining water treatment with wetland management," he said holding up Xeroxed copies of two academic journal articles for her inspection. She looked at them, impressed that Ned had coauthored them.

"Thanks. These will be really helpful, if I don't break my neck before I get down these steps," she sighed at the ease with which Joe had leaped to the ground.

Ned waited while she walked carefully down the steps leaving a trail of drying mud. "Nice legs, Paula," he joked as she scratched off some of the caked dirt on her shin.

"Watch it, buster, or I'll put dirt on your shoes."

He laughed as they walked back to his car, but once they were seated, he turned to her with a serious expression. "Are you ready for this? It's going to be a mess over there."

Paula pressed her lips firmly together and took a

deep breath. "Yes. Let's go get it over with. I'm going to have a lot of work to do."

Three hours later she finally collapsed on a broken wooden chair and accepted a McDonald's bag from Ned. A small pile of damp clothing and a larger pile of damp furniture sat drying in the open air of her roofless living room.

"Thank goodness I found my purse." She sighed and took a bite.

Ned stood gazing at the remains of the apartment and then sat on the floor beside her. "What about important papers? Did you have them here?"

"No. Another blessing, that is. I keep everything in a safe deposit box, and I always go through my clutter here before I start grading finals. It's a long-standing tradition I learned from my mentor teacher. That way, when school is out I actually get a vacation instead of being hit with having to clean my house." She put her chin in her palm and rested her elbow on her knee. "The best-laid plans, and all that, huh."

Just then Ned's pager sounded, and Paula shrugged. "I'm not the only one with problems, Ned Andersen."

He looked at the number printing across the face of the pager and frowned. "That's odd . . . I'll be back, Paula. I can use the phone in the car."

He left and Paula returned to her efforts to sort through her books. The most painful part of the process was tossing out those that were ruined beyond repair. She could hardly bring herself to lose anything else, no matter how damaged it might be. Finally she decided to try again to reach her insurance company, and she walked over to the drugstore across the street to find another phone. Ned was coming toward her with a big smile on his face.

"That was the cavalry! They're on the way with our supplies, ma'am. We don't have to sell the ranch after all!"

"Ned, what are you talking about?"

He continued to grin at her. "That was Sean. He heard about your apartment on the news. He's driving over with some equipment for you."

Paula pulled herself out of the funk into which she had been sinking and managed to return Ned's smile. "Did he say how Sarah's doing?"

"His description was 'holding steady.' I told him I thought you were doing at least that well."

Half an hour later, after a long conversation with her insurance agent, Paula thought she might even be making headway. She started back to the apartment. Her neighbors worked in a similar way, piling up what they could save, occasionally crying over some irreplaceable lost article. Most had friends and relatives helping them, and neighbors from the first floor also helped. The ground level of the building had suffered damage from broken windows, but the second story was nearly demolished from the loss of the roof.

Two other buildings down the street, one a single family home and the other a small bakery, had also lost their roofs where the funnel cloud had approached but never actually touched ground. Paula knew the community was fortunate. Other towns had experienced tornadoes so terrible they leveled every building. Preston's residents had not even suffered any serious injuries. She watched with warm gratitude as Ned carried the front end of a mattress to a pickup truck indicated by her elderly neighbor, Mrs. Strahl. With a start, Paula realized the back end of the mattress was carried by Sean. She hurried across the street to help them.

"Mrs. Strahl, are you leaving?" Paula asked with concern.

"Well, of course, dear. I'm too old to camp out under the stars, and I'm certainly too old to camp out in the rain. My daughter and her husband are taking me to their house in Columbus."

Her words hit Paula with an amazing force. She had nowhere to live. Somehow, all day she had forced herself to cope with each problem as it arose, but she had not allowed herself to grapple with the totality of her loss. Even as she spoke with her insurance agent about the need to handle her emergency expenses, she had not thought of what that meant other than the need to have some clothes and a car.

Ned and Sean watched her open her mouth and freeze. Ned instinctively knew her thoughts, and he put an arm around her and steered her down the sidewalk a little way.

"Come on, Paula, don't lose it now. You're okay. I told you the cavalry was bringing us supplies."

"What?" Paula shook herself out of her stupor. "What did you say?"

"Look," he answered, pointing to a good-sized camper parked next to them. "Your castle awaits you, courtesy of our local squire, Sean Brady."

Paula had seen the Bradys' camper before, and she understood immediately what Ned meant. She turned and found Sean behind them. "How can I ever thank you?"

"You can baby-sit." He laughed. "I wish I could stay longer, but I have a ride waiting at Ned's to take me back home. Good luck, Paula. I'll park it in a place that's nice and protected, next to the hillside on Ned's property. Keep it all summer if you like. That way you can take your time deciding on a place to live. Call if you need anything.'' He jumped in the camper and drove off.

''Close your mouth, Paula. That's just the way he is. He's always giving things to other people as if *things* don't matter to him at all.''

''I would like to be that way, myself. Instead I've been whining about losing a few books.''

''Come on, girl. You've lost more than a few books, and you haven't done any whining at all that I've heard. Why don't you look around in the apartment once more, and I'll bring down that pile of clothes for you.''

Two hours later Paula had arranged storage for her wet, but salvageable belongings and had loaded all her essentials into the back of Ned's car. Too tired to think, and beginning to feel a return of her headache, she closed her eyes as they drove back to his house.

For the first time, she took a good look around her. The house, a pleasant two-story frame building with an old-fashioned wraparound porch, sat nearly a hundred yards off the road to the west of the river. The small cleared area in front of the house showed evidence of a dedicated gardener, but the rest of the lot appeared to be untouched woods. The land rose in a gentle incline that abruptly steepened just to the west of the house. True to his word, Sean had parked the camper close to this bluff so that Paula felt as if she could nestle her back up against that little hill and feel safe from the worst winds.

Ned insisted that she use the shower while he took Hector for a run, and then that she rest on the padded porch swing while he showered himself. She lay sleepily running her fingers through Hector's hair while she listened to the sounds of early evening. This should have been one of the worst days of

Paula's life, but except for a return of her headache, she felt perfectly contented. She had survived a life-threatening disaster, she had worked side by side with neighbors and friends, and now some very kind friends had provided her with as much security as anyone could have in rural Ohio during tornado season.

Of all that she had experienced over the last two days, Paula found most surprising her companionable relationship with Ned. She laughed at herself for her preconceived notions that he would be a finicky person just because he always looked so good. She still thought his orderliness might be a kind of protectiveness, but he certainly didn't distance himself from someone in need. He demonstrated consistent good humor and thoughtfulness toward his employees, her neighbors, and herself. Ned Andersen showed definite possibilities as a good friend.

All right, Paula, she thought. *Be honest. His attractiveness won't be ignored. He shows definite possibilities as much more than a good friend.*

She must have dozed for a while, for the next thing she felt was Ned lightly shaking her shoulder and offering her some iced tea and a salad. They ate out on the porch, Hector keeping his head either on Paula's feet or, when Ned didn't catch him, on her lap. They sat until well after dark, swinging gently on the porch swing and talking about their work and lives.

When Paula finally stood up to leave for the camper, Ned took her hand and gently kissed her on the cheek. "You've been an awfully good sport today, Paula. Not many people can put up with this much trouble without being pretty irritable."

"You've been wonderful, Ned. I don't know what I would have done if you hadn't helped me out."

"Don't you have any family nearby?"

"No. I have one sister in Georgia. My father died when I was in college, and my mother is in a nursing home down near my sister. Normally I would have had a dozen students and teachers to help me, but when school lets out everyone seems to go their own way."

He squeezed her hand once more. "I'm glad I could help."

Alone in her borrowed camper, Paula collapsed from exhaustion without sparing even a minute for worry about her situation or the beginning of another stormy night.

Chapter Six

Early the next morning Ned found her working at her small table, outlining the ecological history of the study area. She had spread out a topographical map across the entire work space and had marked the boundaries and potential working units for a management plan. Today she planned to begin taking soil samples and identifying the vegetative cover already on the field, but first, she wanted to get a history of the drainage system.

"I imagine the previous owner could tell you about every ditch he ever dug to keep that field dry," Ned commented as he accepted the cup of coffee she offered him.

Paula shook her head. "He probably could have done it a few years ago, but I heard that he has Alzheimer's now and has a lot of memory trouble. I'm going to try the son. He's the one who sold the land. There are about seventy-five acres out there, so I'll have a lot of walking to do.

"I'll drive you to the car dealership to pick up your rental first. And I want you to take this." He spoke firmly as he held out a house key. "You're obviously going to need a telephone and a shower. I know this camper has a filing cabinet with a water faucet that they call a shower, but you're going to be dealing with some heavy-duty mud."

"But I can . . ."

"Don't argue, or I won't take you to get your car."

Paula grinned and shook her head at the same time. "You're awfully bossy this morning, Mr. Andersen."

"I know. Take the key."

She took it, grateful not to need to arrange for the use of a telephone. By the time she arrived back at the house that night, she was even more grateful for the use of the shower. When working in the field Paula took precise, clean samples and kept them immaculately well ordered in her sample case. She carried a water supply in her trunk to clean her hands between samples, and she managed not to contaminate one soil with another. But, while she cleaned her hands repeatedly during the day, the rest of her body accumulated examples of dirt from every square foot of the study site.

Paula held a change of clothes and a towel away from her filthy body as she climbed the porch stairs. "Don't say it," she warned Ned, who sat rocking in the porch swing. "Just point me to the hose."

He didn't say anything, but he rose and held the door open for her. She had already removed her shoes and socks, but she felt guilty walking in her dirty bare feet across his clean floor, and she hesitated.

"For crying out loud, Paula. I work with the wastewater of an entire county all day long. Do you really think I'm going to get upset about some nice clean dirt on my floor? You're a lot more obsessed about this cleanliness thing than I am." He pushed her gently inside and returned to his seat.

Once again they shared a meal and talked about their day with the easy intimacy of two people who found each other interesting. Paula's efforts to talk with the son of the previous owner of the site had availed her nothing.

"He apparently never cared about the farm and doesn't much care what happens to the land now," Paula explained to Ned. "He remembered that his father always had a lot of trouble keeping those back acres drained, but he didn't bother to learn what his father did about it."

"We could just lay out a controlled drainage system, like the one we set up at Centerville, and not worry about returning the land to its exact former topography."

They laid out one of Ned's maps, and he began to sketch a series of rectangles representing ponds. They discussed seasonal water levels and the needs of various birds and animals until they both began yawning at the same time.

"Enough!" Ned declared. "We certainly aren't going to finish this entire project in one night. Go home and go to sleep!"

He gently guided her off the porch and toward her trailer, then waved a careless hand as he turned to enter his own house. Paula felt a mild disappointment that there was no good-night kiss, but she just assumed that Ned didn't find her all that attractive.

She also reminded herself that she didn't need a summer romance that might leave her feeling depressed when she returned to teaching in the fall. Besides, friendship had the advantage that it might last; whereas, Paula's romantic relationships had never seemed to last more than a few weeks.

Over the next two weeks they fell into the pattern of meeting for coffee in Paula's trailer in the early morning and sharing dinner on Ned's porch in the evening. Hector began pushing his way into the camper and sometimes remained under Paula's feet when she worked at the table during the day. She made some half-hearted attempts to find a temporary apartment, but finally decided to take Sean's advice and keep the camper until her own apartment building had been repaired. Her work progressed smoothly, and she had less loneliness than she had experienced for the past several summers. Paula decided she believed the old adage about it being truly an ill wind that blew no good and then wondered when she had started thinking in clichés.

Although Paula's headaches stopped after a few days, she continued to experience some disconcerting after-effects of the tornado. Whenever the sky began to darken with storm clouds, her heart would initiate a drumroll of anxiety. Central Ohio always experienced a fair amount of wind; after all, there were no significant geographical barriers to stop it, and Paula watched the treetops as she worked in the field, searching for any change in the wind's direction or intensity.

About a week after moving into the camper, Paula stopped at the store for some groceries to share with Ned for dinner. In spite of being tired from her long hours of hiking, Paula anticipated the evening with pleasure, and she spent some extra time looking for

Ned's favorite brand of coffee. When she finally loaded the bags in the backseat of the car she realized how dark the sky had become. She watched a small flock of sparrows speeding away from the easy crumbs of the street to the sheltering safety of a large stand of trees.

Heart palpitations caused her to tremble as she quickly climbed in behind the steering wheel. She forced herself to maintain the speed limit as she navigated the narrow streets of Preston, but as soon as she passed the city limits she pressed the accelerator to the floor. Whipping along the river road, she could feel her panic rising even faster than the wind. By the time she reached Ned's property, she no longer controlled her actions.

Blindly she opened the door to the trailer, but she couldn't stay there. ''Not safe!'' The words filled her mind. ''Not safe!'' She had to get out of this tiny, unprotected tin can. She ran to the house and began banging on the door. Hector barked excitedly from inside, but apparently Ned had not yet arrived home. Paula searched for the key and vaguely remembered leaving her purse in the camper. She ran back, not even noticing that rain now pelted her along with the wind.

She found the key in her purse on top of the maps she had left spread out on the RV's table and then realized that she had piles of her work scattered all around her temporary home. She had to keep her work safe. She started rolling up maps trying to secure them with rubber bands and paper clips, but each effort took far longer than normal because her fingers wouldn't work. She began shaking from fear and cold, while the wind and rain blew in the open door of the trailer.

Tears streamed down her face, and when a flash

of lightning burst almost simultaneously with a huge clap of thunder, she screamed as if she had been shot. Her world disintegrated to the single experience of terror. Her papers ceased to exist, the key to the house held no meaning, all she knew was the need to hide from this hideous sucking monster that would kill her.

"Paula! Paula, are you all right?" Ned saw the door banging against the side of the trailer in the wind and noticed a stream of papers carried by the wind out across the small lawn. He jumped from his car and entered the camper. "Paula?"

Her work blew around the table, and he started to gather it and weight it down when he heard a whimpering sound coming from under the table. Paula sat curled into an impossibly small space with her arms over her head and her head tucked between drawn up knees.

"Oh, Paula." Ned saw a frightened child in the delicate, terrified form, and he crawled under the table to pull her out.

"No!" She screamed and started to hit him as he dragged her out into the open. "No! It's not safe!" She resisted him with fists, nails, and then feet.

As small as she was, Paula had a fair amount of strength, and Ned wanted to avoid either of them being injured. "It's all right, Paula," he spoke soothingly and stopped pulling on her. He pushed himself completely underneath the table until he sat scrunched up against her. "I won't try to make you move. It's okay. We're here together now. It's safe."

She curled up again, once more covering her head with her arms, and Ned slid his arm around her shoulders protectively. Talking constantly, he rubbed her shoulder and her arm with one hand and stroked her head with the other. He held her closely, and she leaned into the protective curve of his arm. Finally he felt the rigid muscles in her back begin to release their tension and her sharp hyperventilation begin to slow to more normal breathing. He continued to speak and stroke her hair, calming the last of her panic. He felt her sigh, but she left her head between her knees.

"Paula?" he leaned close to her ear and whispered her name.

Paula lifted her head and covered her face with her hands. Still not speaking, she shook her head and then rubbed her face with her hands as if she wanted to clean off some particularly stubborn dirt on her cheeks and forehead. Finally she heaved another great sigh.

"I suppose we ought to get out from under here before you do permanent damage to your spine," she said, sounding exasperated.

Without a word, Ned backed out from under the table, managing to get upright with only one minor bump to his head. Paula slipped out with ease, her spritely figure reminding Ned of an elf emerging from a mushroom hideaway and causing him to grin. But when he saw how she hid her face from him in embarrassment, he sobered immediately.

"Are you all right now?"

"Oh, I'm fine," she responded heatedly. "I'm just a neurotic, storm-phobic who loses her mind when faced with thunder." A deep rumble sounded in the distance, as if the heavens were celebrating their triumph over her.

"You handled that one pretty well," he pointed out.

"Well, I'm not alone at the moment," she sulked. Lifting one of her maps, she shook her head. "Look at this mess. I've probably lost half of my work. What a worthless . . .''

Ned grabbed both of her arms and pulled her around to face him. "Don't. You're an educated woman, Paula. You know what trauma does to a person. Just because you chose not to talk to those emergency counselors, don't expect yourself not to have any aftermath from the tornado.''

Paula acknowledged the truth in his words, and she nodded. But her brain once again refused to operate the way it should. Instead of listening to Ned, Paula's awareness riveted to the warmth of his hands on her arms and the intensity of his brown eyes as they gazed into hers. Through the haze of memory of her panic she suddenly recalled his arm wrapped around her and his hand stroking her hair. His closeness stirred a flush in her cheeks and a tightness in her throat, nearly precipitating another panic attack. Breathing seemed impossible again until suddenly Ned dropped his hands from her arms and reached to pick up some of her papers from the floor.

With a shudder Paula gasped a lung full of air. What had happened here? For a minute she had thought Ned was about to kiss her, but now he exhibited the same detached courtesy he always showed her. He stacked papers, rolled the maps that had come loose from her clumsy attempts to corral them, and grabbed a towel to wipe up the rainwater.

Paula forced her limbs to action and picked up a few papers herself. Glancing out the window, she saw a few of her scattered sheets twisting across the yard.

"Darn it!" she cried, and she pushed out of the camper after her precious notes. In a few minutes Ned joined her and they managed to collect most of what she had lost.

"It's a mess, but I think I can still read it. I should have entered these into the computer. That will teach me to procrastinate." She attempted to laugh at herself as they returned to her work area and secured everything, but the effort fell somewhat short of her goal.

"Hungry?" Ned asked without looking at her.

"Oh, no, my groceries!" Paula moaned. When she retrieved the bags from the back of the car; however, she found that the ice cream had not even melted. It seemed as if hours had passed since she left the store, but in fact it had only been about thirty minutes. The process of carrying the food into Ned's kitchen, and adequately greeting the desperate Hector, allowed them to pass over whatever embarrassment lingered from those few moments in the trailer. By the time they had eaten they were able to sit on the porch listening to the steady rain with at least a good imitation of their familiar level of comfort.

For Paula the encounter during the storm floated just below her conscious thoughts during the next few days, and when she sat quietly for even a few minutes the memory would drift to the surface leaving her confused and slightly troubled. She knew herself well enough to recognize a serious attraction when she felt it, but something warned her that Ned did not feel the same way. He certainly had not pressed for anything physical between them and seemed perfectly content to remain friends. Paula thought she ought to be pleased with any relationship based on such mutual respect and enjoyment, but she worried that her physical attraction to Ned might result in feelings of rejection since he didn't reciprocate. Well, she would just have to watch out for herself.

Ned's reaction to the storm consisted of battening

down his emotional hatches. Late into the night he had paced through the house, searching for some activity to engage the energy coursing through his body. He felt the heaviness of his eyelids closing, but as soon as he lay down, he saw Paula's face as she had turned toward him that afternoon. He remembered the play of shadows across her cheeks, the shining curls lightly touching her ears and neck, the softness of her skin over the tightness in her arm muscles. Then his thoughts would return to the feel of her back beneath his arm and the soft sweetness of her hair as he stroked it.

Slamming his fist down on his mattress, he stood again ready to pace once more. The house was spotless, testimony to many nights such as this one, when Ned used activity instead of sleeping pills to find oblivion. Before Paula, the sleepless nights were owed to his memories of Annie, and those times of loneliness and loss had become so familiar he hardly acknowledged them. But this restlessness carried its own unique quality, almost as if he had a goal or prize to reach, and his body wouldn't let him rest until he had achieved it. This restlessness carried the quality of hope, and that was one feeling Ned had long ago learned to recognize as the enemy.

Crossing the living room, Ned leaned against the mantel and stared at Annie's photograph without lifting it from its place. He looked at her smiling face, remembering her laughter and the way she would tease him out of a bad mood. He shook his head. No, that wasn't right. Annie would just tell him to get over it. Paula was the one who would tease him, comparing him to herself on one of her bad days. But Annie had laughed a lot, just like Paula. Both had the ability to find the humor in the worst situations.

He amused himself thinking about the differences between them. Paula would go rushing off through the mud and brush, carrying a scoop net and searching for mayfly larvae to prove the health of her wetlands, and totally unconcerned about her destroyed sneakers. Annie would have insisted on wearing wading boots if she had been forced out of her laboratory for fieldwork. But both of them would work until they dropped to keep a system healthy. Annie would have had the new plant owner over for dinner and softened up like melted butter before trying to work on the ecosystem. Paula just rushed into battle, assuming that anyone she didn't know was probably the enemy.

What was he doing? Why was he thinking this way? He needed to go wax the car or something! He needed to quit thinking about Paula. A distant flash of lightning followed several seconds later by the roll of thunder mocked his efforts to escape himself as his thoughts immediately raced with concern about Paula. *No,* he said solemnly to himself. *I will not do this.*

Lifting Annie's picture, he carried it back upstairs to his room and placed it on the table beside his bed. "I love you, Annie. I will love you forever." He repeated the phrase he had spoken to her every night of their married life. Over and over he said the words, until finally, returned to the familiar feel of dull loss, he fell asleep.

Paula's disgust with her anxiety pushed her to overcome it, and she hoped that her fear of storms had disappeared when she managed to sit through one while swinging on Ned's porch one evening. They had finished eating and watched the clouds roll in while they talked about their early lives. Paula had been describing how she kept a birdhouse with her and hung it outside every house her family had lived in. "The only problem was, that we moved so often, the birds never really had a chance to use it." She sighed, looking over her shoulder at the darkening sky. The first rumbling of thunder started Paula's heart skipping with heightened anxiety.

"So what did you think thunder was when you were a child, Paula?" Ned wrenched her attention back to him.

"My mother always told me it was the angels bowling, but she said rain came from the angels taking a shower, so I voiced scepticism fairly early on. After all, even angels wouldn't be likely to bowl in the shower!"

He laughed at her. "A scientist from the beginning?"

"Well, what about you? What did you think it was?"

"I was a scientist, too. My father gave me a technical explanation of thunder and lightning one time when I was very frightened. After that I knew exactly what caused the problem. The people driving the clouds were running into each other, and the noise was from the collisions! I remember worrying that they would fall out of the sky and land on me."

"My sister thought that the giant from *Jack and the Beanstalk* had dropped his marbles. I always liked that explanation."

As they laughed, the storm came closer and the wind picked up, twisting the leaves on the silver maple trees in Ned's yard. A blinding flash of lightning illuminated the drive down to the river and the immediate crash of thunder jolted Paula from the swing. Her voice trembled as she strove to continue the conversation while pacing the length of the porch.

"Do you have any brothers or sisters, Ned?"

He heard the quaver in her words and grabbed her hand as she passed his chair. "Yes, I do. Sit back down and I'll tell you about my eight younger siblings."

"Eight!" The shock of learning about Ned's large family nearly drove the panic from Paula's mind.

He pulled her back to the swing and sat beside her, still holding her hand. He began listing the family tree while he rocked the swing gently. "I'm the oldest. I'm Edward. Then there is my sister Elizabeth, who has three children, Michael, Nora, and Allen. Then comes Eric with his son, Trevor. Then Emory. He's never been married. Then the twins Frances and Amanda. Mother apparently ran out of E names by the time the twins came along. And isn't it strange that only Emory uses his E. I'm Ned, and then there's Lizzy, and Rick. After the twins came . . ."

Paula listened to the litany of siblings, trying to remember them all, but losing track with no faces to accompany the names. Ned rubbed his thumb slowly across the back of her hand as he talked, and she found herself totally distracted from the progressing storm. By the time he had finished naming his first degree relatives, Paula found herself profoundly relaxed and actually enjoying the beauty of the storm. Ned's warm, dry hand spread comfort through her entire body, and she closed her eyes contentedly.

"What was it like, being the oldest of so many children?" Paula asked sleepily.

Ned chuckled a little. "I learned how to be responsible. You like to tease me about how neat I am, but it's a direct consequence of trying to fend off the chaos of eight kids. My mother made us all toe the line, and as the oldest, I was her first lieu-

tenant. I guess I can still be kind of bossy sometimes, but I prefer to think of it as leadership.''

''You're a caretaker, aren't you?'' It wasn't really
a question. She knew him well enough to recognize
his need to help others, including herself.

Ned remained silent for a few minutes. ''I know
that that has negative connotations these days, but
when I was growing up, taking care of others was
considered a good thing, especially for an eldest
son.''

''I wasn't criticizing, Ned, just acknowledging
it.''

''Yes, well, I guess you're right. I'm a caretaker.''

''Do you ever let anyone take care of you?'' She
turned to face him in the gathering darkness, very
aware that he still held her hand.

He also seemed to realize that he had continued
to keep hold of her hand, even after she clearly no
longer needed the calming effect of his touch. He
stopped the rhythmic movement of his thumb and
opened his fingers to release her. Standing in a fluid
movement that spoke to Paula of a need to escape,
he coughed and said, ''That's the hard part, isn't
it?''

Paula recognized an exit line when she heard one,
and she also stood. ''Thanks, Ned. I think I must be
over the worst part of my reactions to storms. Just
in time for the dry spell we're supposed to be getting
next week!'' Laughing to cover her sudden embarrassment, she waved good night and returned to the
camper. This time she wondered if Ned's detach-
ment from her sprang from true indifference or
something else.

The next morning she found that the previous
night's storm had done some significant damage to

the birdhouses at the preserve. Fortunately, most of the fledglings had left home, and the second round of breeding had not begun in earnest; however, three house poles had been blown over, and Paula spent a considerable amount of time replacing them. By the time she crossed over to the plant site, she wasn't at all surprised to see that a number of dead trees had been blown down. She again saw the signs of wren nesting in the damaged trunks and realized that the tiny birds would be out looking for new sites.

Spying several of the tiny brown creatures in a nearby ash tree, she called up to them. "You're just like me, Jenny Wren. Blown out of house and home. Don't worry, your husband will take care of you." He would, too, as Paula knew. The male wren would build dummy nests all around the area and show the sites to his lady until she selected one to finish for their children's home. Paula shook her head in surprise, realizing that the thought of the helpful male wren had brought to mind a picture of Ned helping her gather up her windblown papers.

At the end of her second week of work, Paula and Ned rode together to Centerville for another dinner with Sarah and Sean. Paula carried her preliminary report for Sean, and she hoped it would result in something positive for the study area. Her evaluation of the land clearly indicated that the depression on the eastern side of the field would revert to wetlands if drainage was discontinued. Already, after only one fallow season, the field showed signs of vegetation and wildlife that had escaped from the swamp in the preserve. In spite of substantial use of insecticides, the farmer had not damaged the natural health of the area, and Paula had begun cataloguing evidence of abundant birds, game, and invertebrates in the area.

When she showed her report to Sean and Sarah

that evening, she asked hopefully, "Is there any chance that we could convert this one section into a wildlife management section? Even with the plant near, we could do so much."

Sarah started laughing, much to Paula's chagrin. "Oh, Paula, don't look so disheartened. I'm only laughing because you haven't been around these two enough. They're going to tell you that the problem with your suggestion is that you aren't thinking big enough."

Paula looked at both Ned and Sean as they nodded at Sarah's words. Sean leaned over the map and pointed to spot after spot saying, "What about the good prairie space here? And here? And this stand of hemlocks is much too well developed to lose. We'd be displacing all sorts of wildlife."

"But how can you save all of that space and still have enough room for the facility? What about parking for the employees? What about your water treatment facilities, Ned?" Paula worried that Sean's suggestions were too unrealistic to have any value at all.

Sean didn't speak but opened a small notebook and began jotting down words along the left side of a page. Occasionally he flipped to another page and sketched a quick diagram that meant nothing to Paula. She felt left out of a silent communication passing between these three friends who had worked together so often.

Sarah reached for her friend's hand and squeezed it. "This is a wonderful preliminary report, Paula. We need to understand exactly what's available before we can make any suggestions. The developer may not want to listen to a plan that asks him to give up any of his land, but a plan that suggests the best, comprehensive use of the entire place may be well received.''

Paula looked doubtful, but this time Ned challenged her preconceptions. "Remember, Paula, we're dealing with an ethanol production plant, not a steel mill. This is a 'green industry' if ever there was one. A major thrust for ethanol production was to free us from dependence on fossil fuels, but there are a lot of environmental reasons for using biomass products. The emissions are radically less than with gasoline, and the waste is almost nonexistent.''

Sarah added, "The biggest problem these guys face is how to make enough profit to keep their plants operating. The last ethanol producer in Ohio went out of business, as I recall.''

Sean nodded. "But some of the larger companies in Nebraska and Kansas are doing very well, and the Canadian producers are thriving. Sometimes, it's a matter of starting up a business at the right time to capitalize on the best technology and still hit the market early enough to get in before someone else has it cornered.''

Paula wondered how her study of the plant site would fit in if it meant any extra expense for a marginal industry. When she voiced her concerns, Ned smiled conspiratorially. "We'll just have to make it worth his while. Remember, the county has the right of imminent domain. We can buy the land from him for a treatment plant, if we really need to. But I think we'll be able to work something out.''

"Don't let them worry you, Paula," Sarah commiserated. "After a while you'll get sucked into the politics of it all, just like I did. The amazing thing is that it can actually be beneficial.''

"If you say so," Paula mumbled. "Come on, Hector. What you and I both need is something tangible to chase.'' She raced the dog around in the yard for a while before returning to find Sean just putting away her materials.

''I think I'll pay a visit to the developer next week and see what we might come up with,'' he said as he handed Paula her file. ''In the meantime, I would like for you to finish your impact study with an added emphasis on how to manage that property. I want you to include the various needs of the wildlife and the humans who will be using the space. Let your imagination run wild and pretend that cost is no object. We'll have plenty of time to be realistic later.''

''Whatever you say, boss.'' Paula knew she would have no trouble filling the request, but she doubted that her plans would ever be enacted.

Sarah began to look tired soon after they had eaten, so Paula and Ned left early. Every day Paula felt more confused around Ned. They had only known each other for a little more than a month, but they had spent so much time together that Paula felt as if she knew him better than she had ever known any man. All the good impressions she had formed since the tornado remained after two weeks of their close living arrangements, and she saw no sign that he would suddenly change into someone else. On the other hand, she worried that she continued to feel so strongly attracted to him when he didn't seem to share those feelings. He showed no sign that he had felt anything after the afternoon of her panic attack, and Paula concluded after the last storm that he had comforted her only as he would have comforted anyone in that position.

As they drove back along the dark country roads, Paula unconsciously heaved a sigh as she recognized her disappointment that this relationship would probably remain just one more of the many acquaintances she seemed to collect.

"Is everything all right?" Ned asked quietly in the darkness.

"What?" She jerked her thoughts back to the present.

"You sighed so hard you sounded kind of sad."

Paula blushed and was grateful for the darkness. "I didn't even realize it. I think I must be kind of tired."

He looked at her briefly before turning his attention back to the road. "I hope you didn't feel like I was intruding on your work tonight. I've done so many of these projects with Sean that I didn't stop to think that this is really your baby. I'm sorry if I got in your way."

Paula stared at him in amazement. "No. I didn't feel that way at all. We've talked about this every day for two weeks, Ned. I feel like you're as involved as I am, almost like a partner. I appreciated your input."

She saw his shoulders and arms relax and realized he had been extremely tense until that moment. With a shock she understood how closely he guarded all of his emotions. Perhaps what she had felt as a companionable intimacy had been nothing more than a detached act of charity for a victim of the tornado. How would she even know if he resented her living on his property? After all, it had been Sean's suggestion, not Ned's.

He said something that she missed as she let her concern mount. "What? I didn't hear you."

"I said I'm glad. I wouldn't want to do anything to hurt you."

Now she felt totally confused. This sounded like true friendship, and his voice carried a tone of warmth she hadn't heard before. Or was this just more of those good manners and caretaking his mother had taught him? In frustration Paula decided she actually was very tired, and she would do well to just go home and go to sleep.

When they parted at the driveway, Ned gave her a lingering look before walking up the steps to his house. Hector insisted that she give him a kiss before he followed his master. *I have a lot better luck with dogs,* Paula thought. *I probably ought to get one.*

Chapter Seven

Just before dawn Hector paid her an unexpected visit. Scratching at her door and barking, he announced his own presence before she heard a very human knock and Ned's voice.

"Paula? You have a phone call."

Suddenly she came completely awake, filled with terror that her mother might have taken a turn for the worse. She flung open the door to see Ned standing there calmly holding his cordless phone out to her. The look on her face must have frightened him, for he reached out and touched her on the cheek.

"It's all right. This isn't bad news," he said in that soothing voice he had used on her before.

She immediately calmed down and, still standing in the doorway, took the phone from him.

"Paula?"

"Sarah! Are you all right?"

"I'm great. I'm a mother!"

Paula listened to her friend describe the birth of her son, Kevin, and felt tears falling down her cheeks as she heard Sarah's awe of the event. Ned stood close to her, smiling as he watched her hear what he had already heard. When she finally broke the connection, she found him only inches from her, the height of the step bringing her face even with his.

Her heart beat rapidly, and she felt a sensation of heat rush from her heart to her throat. "I . . . I . . . isn't it great?" She thrust the phone at him and watched in confusion as he reached behind her to set it down on the floor of the camper. The movement brought him even closer to her, and he did not draw back.

"You're great," Ned whispered. "You are so beautiful I can hardly bear to look at you."

Where had this come from? Paula felt overwhelmed by Ned's sudden intense scrutiny after a month of apparent disinterest. In self-defense she had stifled her feelings for him because she instinctively identified his reticence, but now he openly expressed the same attraction that pulled at her. She didn't care what had held him back before, as long as she could feel this incredible warmth now.

He reached for her cheek the way he had done earlier and turned her face to his. Softly his lips pressed into hers, coaxing her to lean into him. His hand moved behind her head and his fingers combed through her short, tumbled hair. Taking her head in both hands, he kissed her harder, and Paula wrapped both of her arms around him, willing him to kiss her like this forever.

His lips brushed her eyes, her temple, and her ear, and she heard him murmuring as he pressed his fingers through her hair. "This is so right. It is so right.'' She agreed with her whole heart, and she willingly kissed him back.

Finally Paula loosened her arms and placed her hands on Ned's chest, giving him a gentle shove. He pulled back slightly, looking deeply into her eyes. He didn't say anything, but Paula felt as if he were more relaxed than she had ever seen him. She knew they couldn't stand here kissing like this, or she would find things moving much faster than she wanted, but she couldn't let him leave yet, either.

''I'll make us some coffee,'' she offered, clearing her throat twice just to get the words out.

He nodded, still not speaking or moving until Paula pushed again on his chest and moved away from him into the camper. Then he let Hector jump up before him into the tiny kitchen.

Paula took her time with the coffee, but neither of them spoke until she had two mugs and the table between them. Then, as she played with the handle of her steaming mug, Ned reached across the table and traced his index finger over the back of her hand.

''Well,'' he said, his eyes seeming to light up with mischief.

''Well,'' she responded. Paula wasn't going to do the talking for both of them.

He cleared his throat and grinned self-consciously. ''I guess this has been building up for a while.''

''I guess so.'' She grinned, too.

''You didn't mind? I mean, you . . .'' His voice trailed off as if he didn't know how to say what he meant. Instead of continuing, he turned her hand over and trailed his finger up the inside of her wrist. Paula gasped at the sensuous chill that traveled all the way to her shoulder.

She pulled her arm away, reluctantly but insistently. ''Of course I didn't mind. You know that.

I'm a little overwhelmed, and I don't want to rush into anything. I'd like to take this slowly.''

He nodded and stood up. "I think you're right. I'd better get back. It's already morning and we've both got work to do.'' They stared at each other for a few minutes until suddenly Paula started giggling. They were back in each others' arms in a second, laughing like two children who have discovered a wonderful new game. She felt as if she had come home. His arms around her, his heart beating strongly beneath her head as she leaned against his chest, the warmth of his breath against the top of her head, all enveloped her with a glow and security she hadn't even known she lacked. Finally she shoved him out the door, with the promise that she would try to finish her work early.

Ned took the steps three at a time, feeling younger than he had in years. He radiated energy as he rushed through his work that day, completely surprising his secretary, Grace, when he laughed aloud at one of the lab technician's jokes. Since she had worked for Ned, Grace had never seen him bad tempered, but she had also never heard him laugh. Some of his older friends at the plant remembered a humorous side to their boss, which had been conspicuously absent since his wife first became ill, and a few raised knowing eyebrows as they watched him now.

Ned tried not to let himself think too much about exactly what it was he felt toward Paula. When he was with her he knew he relaxed and enjoyed himself. He realized he had not laughed so much for nearly six years, and he knew he wanted the feelings to continue. Arriving at home that evening, he raced through the house, practically chasing Hector out the door for his run, and then rushing through his shower so he could meet Paula at her car when she arrived home.

"Let's go out to eat," he said before he even said hello. "You know, like a date."

"A date!" She laughed. "What an original idea. I like it."

While she changed, he paced around the yard, charged with an energy reminiscent of his nighttime restlessness, but filled with happiness instead of loneliness. When they finally settled in the car to leave, he reached across to pull her to him for a kiss.

"Hello," he whispered into her hair. "I've missed you all day."

Paula's heart skipped a beat at the tenderness of his words, and she knew with absolute certainty that all of her efforts to protect herself were now worthless. This man held her heart in his hands, and he had the power to cause her great pleasure or great pain. She felt the gentle touch of his lips to hers, and she knew he would never purposely hurt her.

To Paula's amazement, their relationship continued smoothly over the next three weeks. She had had so many flirtations over the years that she had come to expect any initial attraction to last about a week. But this connection to Ned felt nothing like a flirtation. They maintained the same working relationship, but Ned's tenderness never diminished. He would look at her in silence for long periods, as if he expected her to disappear, and then reach out to touch her hand or cheek. Paula knew she was falling more deeply in love with him as each day passed, and she could tell he felt the same way. They laughed together easily, and Hector would run back and forth between them, shivering with delight.

Occasionally Ned felt a twinge of something almost like guilt about caring so much for a woman who was not Annie, but he banished those feelings and repaired the cracks in his sense of happiness. If he sat in the living room, Annie's picture sometimes brought a vague feeling of reproach, and for the first time since her death, he found himself avoiding looking at the photo. When the feelings of conflict became too strong, he would resort to his old habit of finding something to keep himself preoccupied until the feelings passed.

He came to Paula's camper each morning for their usual coffee, but instead of eating at the house in the evening, he took her out to dinner at a small local diner. Paula felt as if she were being courted, but in fact she missed the relaxed evenings on the porch. The change in their relationship had opened them to each other, but had somehow placed a boundary around the house. Instead, they made a cozy nest in the corner booth of the restaurant.

Paula had collected an impressive catalogue of wildlife on the study site, and she had begun to understand the needs of an ethanol production plant. Each night they would sit at the diner, and she would review with Ned her results and get his input on the space requirements. When they returned to the cabin, he would kiss her good night at the car rather than invite her to sit for a while on the porch swing. She had said she wanted to go slowly, and maybe this was the best way to avoid the temptation of spending too much time in each others' arms. The temptation certainly existed, since Paula had never before experienced such feelings of longing and belonging.

Energized by the emotional zest in her life, Paula discovered a heightened creativity in her work. As she began evaluating the land use for the plant site, she realized that if the owner approved of her plans, Ned might not even be faced with the prospect of a new treatment facility. This led to the realization that Sean's company would then be out a substantial amount of business, and she came to a crashing halt in her ideas.

Ned intervened at that point and urged her to continue. "Sean asked for your best ideas. He'll decide whether or not to move on them, but he won't want you to limit yourself just so he can make a profit. Surely *you* won't put MER's corporate profits ahead of the needs of the environment!''

Paula might have felt embarrassed by Ned's assessment of her, but he spoke with such humor that she couldn't feel bad. With his encouragement she pressed on until she began to see a cohesive design that actually might satisfy everyone. Time after time, she returned to the land to measure and judge the impact of a particular type of construction, and frequently Ned would join her there, adding his own insights. Those times out in the field held a special magic, as if Ned and Paula could throw off all their other concerns and merge their respective talents into something greater than either one alone. Paula cherished those afternoons more than any other time the couple spent together.

Together they bought a gift for Kevin, a crib mobile with accurately colored songbirds that played their songs when it was wound. The baby became very still as he listened to the calls and crossed his large blue eyes in an effort to watch the movement, suddenly kicking out with both legs in pleasure. Standing in the nursery with his arm around Paula, Ned felt an indescribable sensation in his chest that nearly sent him running from the room. He wanted to pull Paula closer, to hold her to him and say, *Let us have this, too,* but he simultaneously felt an unexplained anxiety and irritation.

He hated to believe that he would react with an adolescent fear toward commitment and responsibility, but he wondered if that was what made him so uncomfortable. Feeling somewhat self-conscious about the stereotype of men who are uncomfortable around babies, he forced himself to remain watching Kevin until he successfully quelled his anxiety. He thought that would be the end of the problem, but he was wrong.

After one particularly long afternoon alone, Paula dragged herself back to her camper, lugging a set of diagrams of soaking tanks and dry and wet mill machinery. The information might be the key to benefitting MER as well as the plant. She had spent the day in the library gathering details about profitable ethanol fuel production, and she didn't want to take a step off this property again tonight. So while Ned and Hector were taking their run, Paula walked to the porch to flop down on the swing. She hadn't had the chance to relax with its lulling rhythm for nearly three weeks.

When man and dog returned, she pleaded fatigue and insisted that they not go out to eat. Ned hesitated, but not understanding his own reluctance to say at home, he shrugged and agreed to fix something on the grill.

"I don't mind doing the cooking, Ned. I can even fix something out in the camper if you'd like," she offered, wondering if he had been feeling imposed on when they ate here.

"No, no. I'll get it. Let me start the grill, and you can help with a salad in a little while."

She relaxed back on the swing while Hector followed Ned into the house. She listened to the familiar sounds from the kitchen, the rattling of drawers and Ned's constant chatter to the dog. *I could so easily settle in here permanently,* she thought contentedly as she listened to Ned moving in and out to the grill.

"Hector, I can't play with you right now." Ned laughed, pushing the retriever out of his way for the third time. Having ignored his initial discomfort about staying home, he now became aware of a lighthearted and energized love of life that he seemed to remember from a distant past. He recognized this feeling, this ecstasy with no more cause than just the joy of being alive with the woman he loved. He closed his eyes, seeing her red-gold hair, her bright blue eyes. From deep within, a hidden memory of being here like this surfaced with inexpressible pleasure.

Hector shoved the tennis ball against Ned's leg again. "No, Hector. You big goof." Ned laughed again. "Go play out front. Take the ball to Annie." Hector stood, head cocked but not moving. "Go on, Hector. Go to Ann. . . ." He stopped cold as he realized what he had said. The wall of denial that had only shown cracks before crumbled with a terrible suddenness as he recognized the conflict in his heart. Pain burst through his tightly constructed barricade with an intensity greater than anything he had felt since he first heard Annie's diagnosis.

On the porch, Paula waited. She had heard the slip and held herself in a precariously balanced space while she waited for what would follow. Had it been merely a slip of the tongue? Anyone could do that. It would be natural for Ned occasionally to confuse the names of two women he loved. But if it was only that, he would be able to handle it with his usual good humor.

Still she waited. Finally she heard Ned speak very quietly to Hector, and the dog pushed open the door

to drop his ball at her feet. She threw a few passes
for Hector to retrieve, but still Ned did not appear
or make a sound from inside. With her heart in her
throat Paula opened the door and passed through to
the kitchen.

"Ned?"

He stood motionless at the sink, leaning on his
hands with his head down.

"Ned?" Paula moved to his side and touched his
arm.

He whipped around as if electrified by her touch,
appalling her with the anguish on his face. Nothing
had prepared her for his look of abject misery and
guilt. Backing away from her he tried to explain,
"Paula . . ." But words failed him.

Paula wanted to hold him, to comfort him, to let
him know that she understood how difficult this was,
but she could see that the closer she stood, the more
miserable he felt. He wanted her gone. Or at least
he wanted her out of this house that held so much
of his beloved Annie. Paula had no right to be in
this home that was meant for the lovely woman
whose picture still graced the mantel.

Paula backed away herself, slivers of ice piercing
her limbs and nearly freezing her to immobility.
With each movement she knew that she left a piece
of her heart behind, but she steeled herself for what
she needed to do.

"I don't really feel like eating now after all," she
started. "In fact I . . . want to put a few things away
in the trailer. I . . . I've decided that it's time I gave
it back to Sean." Her words picked up speed as she
continued. "I'll be finished with my first report in
another week, and I think I might go visit my sister
before school starts. Georgia in August ought to be
hot enough even for me. . . . You know how it is

with us party girls, always looking for the hot spots. Spending the summer in Preston isn't exactly my idea of a good time, you know? I mean, this has been nice and everything, but after a while all this healthy living gets to me.''

She didn't want to babble; she wanted to state her position clearly, but she felt the beginning of despair welling up in her chest. She forced the words she knew she must say. "Ned, this isn't going to work.'' She would retain the upper hand. She would not suffer the humiliation she saw waiting for her if she tried to convince him to give their relationship a chance. "I may have spent a wild and frivolous youth, but even in my craziest moments I had one standard that I never broke. . . . I'm not going to break that rule now. . . . You are the most wonderful person I have ever known, but I promised myself I would never get involved with a married man.'' With that, Paula reached out to touch his arm in one final farewell. His slight flinch confirmed that she had made the correct decision, and she fled back to her tiny home.

It didn't take her long to run away even farther. Within a day she was relocated on a campsite at the Hadley Reservoir, where she told herself her sleeplessness was due to her anxiety about tornadoes rather than any grief she felt about Ned. She shut out everything except her work, finished her final report for MER, and called Mark Jackson to arrange its delivery. She learned then that Sean had been trying to reach her, so she agreed to take the report to Centerville and hand-deliver it to him.

Several hours later, comforted by the warmth of tiny Kevin Brady curled on her chest, and Sarah's good common sense, Paula finally let loose of the tears she had been holding.

"Paula, are you sure you and Ned can't work something out?" Sarah wondered. "Both of you seemed so happy. You just fit together so well."

Paula shook her head sadly. "There really isn't anything to work out. We don't have some irreconcilable differences. . . . Ned's still in love with Annie."

Sarah raised her eyebrows in a silent question and Paula continued. "I think he cares for me. He might even have loved me, if he didn't love her."

"But Annie has been dead for five years!"

"Not to Ned. I have the feeling she has been alive in his heart all this time. I can't compete with that. I don't even want to." Paula's tears started again. "How could I possibly want to hurt a love that deep? Ned's commitment is one of the things I love the most about him, but it's the thing that will keep us apart. Maybe someone else will help him forget her. Not me."

The women sat silently together, Paula grateful for the baby's presence as a distraction from her sadness. His head, damp from the summer heat, pressed against her neck, giving her more pleasure and comfort than she could possibly be giving him. By the time Sean arrived home, Paula's self-control had returned, and she showed him her final report without any signs of distress.

"Paula, I think this is great. Your suggestion for putting the soaking tanks and the yeast vats underground is brilliant."

She forced herself to pretend some pleasure at the compliment. "I know it will mean tearing up the area during construction, but that place is so full of life even after years of farming that I think you'll have about seventy-five percent recovery within two years of the end of construction."

"You've kept most of the topography intact this way."

"Keeping the soaking tanks underground helps maintain a cooler temperature, too, and that reduces refrigerating costs, since the soaking tanks need to be kept at around fifty-nine degrees Fahrenheit."

"Okay. What about waste products?"

"That's one of the major problems. With the use of sulphur dioxide as a soaking agent, the owner can substantially increase his yield and perhaps maintain profitability, but the sulphur dioxide needs to be cleaned out of the water. Ned . . ." She stumbled on his name in spite of her best intentions, but she forced herself to carry on. "Ned assured me we could use a moat system similar to his to carry the water to the wetland area once the water is purified, but the costs of purification may be too high for the owner to bear. On the other hand, if they solve the sulphur dioxide problem, MER won't need to sell much in the way of water treatment equipment other than pumps. The plant will be able to use its own ethanol to fuel pumps and carry the waste to the Centerville plant." She laughed a little. "Ned was right about this being a very 'green' industry. It produces a renewable fuel and utilizes more of the corn than just about anything else."

"Don't worry about MER," Sean said. "According to your notes, our company may be able to sell him the skimmers for the soaking tubs. They look almost identical to our sludge skimmers, and the tubs are certainly the same as the aeration pools. What a fantastic job! We'll present this to the owner tomorrow. I've already arranged for us to meet with him to identify problems and begin looking for solutions."

"I don't have to go with you, do I?" she asked

in alarm. "I thought you were going to do that part."

"But you know that land. You've spent six weeks practically living there, and you can describe it better than anyone else. I think you should meet the owner, anyway. He's not the ogre you've imagined."

With a sigh Paula agreed to go with Sean. Somehow she could manage one more day. "But as soon as this is over, I'm leaving. I'm spending the rest of the summer with my sister in Georgia. My apartment is supposed to be repaired by the last week of August, and I want to be able to go straight in when I return. As grateful as I am for the loan of your camper, I want to have my own kitchen and shower back."

Sean nodded. "I understand you're out at the reservoir now. Are you hoping Georgia will prove that 'absence makes the heart grow fonder?' "

"My life seems to have become a series of clichés, but in this case I think the appropriate one is 'out of sight, out of mind.' "

"Are you all right?"

"No . . . but I'll survive."

Chapter Eight

Survival became Paula's goal over the next few weeks. She had actually enjoyed the presentation with Sean, and she had been very impressed with Parker Mills. His larger concern was profitability, of which he had very little margin, but he embraced her suggestions with enthusiasm and even suggested reducing the size of the parking lot. "If spaces are tight, people may be willing to carpool." However, once the excitement of success wore off, Paula plunged into a depression centered entirely on missing Ned. She flew to Savannah and vegetated at her sister's beachfront property until it was time to return for the opening of school.

Paula's mother lived in a nearby nursing home where she received assistance because of debilitating osteoporosis. Ruth Rosewood's mind remained crystal clear, and she dealt with her constant pain with a sarcastic wit. Paula idolized her mother and missed her terribly. John Rosewood had been a career military man, and the family had moved to a number of places during Paula's childhood. The lack of a hometown never bothered her, but when she completed college and found her first teaching position in Preston, Paula realized she didn't want to move again.

John and Ruth had fallen in love with Savannah several years before John's retirement, and they had considered settling in that gentle Southern city. When Paula's sister, Joan, married a Savannah businessman, the widowed Ruth recovered her fond memories and moved there herself. Now, with her family finally in a permanent place and her own life in a shambles, Paula wondered if she should consider uprooting herself and moving here to be with them.

"Paula, don't be an idiot." Her mother spoke with her usual scarcity of sympathy and abundance of good sense. "You have been telling me for years how much you love your work and your friends. Preston is home to you. Why would you leave it?"

"To be near you? Is that an unreasonable thing for me to want?"

"Well of course not. I'm sure all sensible people would want to be near me if they could. But surely visiting a couple of times a year is enough."

Paula felt tears filling her eyes and tried to blink them back. "Mama, I'm lonely. I want a family. I love my work, but sometimes it's not enough."

"So are you saying there aren't any men living in Ohio? Why don't you get married? I thought from your phone calls this summer that you had found somebody."

"It didn't work out."

"So." Ruth raised an eyebrow in skepticism.

"Others haven't worked out, too, but you didn't come running to Mama saying you want to move to Georgia."

"This one was different." With a relief born from the need to unburden her heart, Paula poured out the entire story while her mother listened and patted her daughter's hand. When she finished, Paula watched her mother's calm, beautiful face, waiting for her reaction.

"You love him very much, don't you?" Ruth asked.

Paula nodded silently.

"We don't give up on the people we love."

"But, Mama, I can't make him love me."

Ruth shook her head forcefully. "Of course not. Love doesn't force people. If you truly love him, you will accept him as he is."

"I tried to do that, Mama. But he couldn't even talk to me. I have to get away from him, put him out of my mind."

"Maybe. Or maybe he needs you to be his friend. He sounds like a hurt and lonely man, Paula. If you were in his place, wouldn't you want your friends to stand by you?"

"I don't know how to do it, Mama."

"If you really love him, you'll find a way. Just don't stop trying until you know that what you're doing is the right thing. You said you didn't want the humiliation of begging for his love, and I don't blame you for that. But don't let your own pride prevent you from making every effort to work things out. If leaving your home and job is the right way to be loving to this man and to yourself, then you need to be sure. Right now, I think it is just running away."

Paula wrapped her arms around her mother's fragile bones and squeezed her gently. She would never understand how so delicate and breakable a body could house such tremendous strength, but she knew with absolute certainty that she was blessed to have such a parent.

Early September found her once more back in her familiar place, touching up lesson plans and roaming Hadley Nature Preserve as a volunteer. Continuing with her study, she wandered over the plant site, searching carefully for habitat that would be used by the wintering animals. No construction could begin until ODNR gave its approval, but surveyors had begun their preliminary work one afternoon when Paula arrived for one of her frequent visits.

She parked away from the surveying equipment and was replacing her teaching shoes with a pair of boots when she heard her name being shouted. "Paula? Paula Rosewood?"

Looking up she saw Parker Mills striding across the field toward her. His welcoming smile drove away any worry that she might be intruding, and he greeted her like a long-lost friend. "I've been hoping to see you again," he started. "I'm concerned about those wetlands of yours." Talking nonstop, he roamed with her over the familiar land, now changed so radically as the seasons progressed.

Parker worried that the bottomlands continued to drain too rapidly, but Paula assured him that seasonal changes were normal and that autumn could claim to be the only dry season in central Ohio. She offered to return and take samples of the mud to check on the health of its microorganisms and to draw up some plans for a bluebird trail like the one at the preserve.

"My real concern is the continuing problems with

the sulphur dioxide waste." Parker looked forlorn. "I just don't know how we're going to manage it, and I haven't been able to get a clear answer from Ned Andersen."

Paula checked her slight start at the mention of Ned's name and responded to Parker's worry. "I'm sure Ned wants to help you out, Parker. He's probably been busy."

"Would you mind talking to him for me, Paula? I know that you can explain the problems I'm up against here. He might be more willing to talk to you."

"I really don't think that's necessary, Parker." Paula felt trapped as she listened to Parker's earnest appeal. "Just give him a call."

"Please, Paula. You aren't tainted by any vested interest in seeing this plant go in. In fact, I know you didn't want it here in the first place. If you ask Ned to help me, I'm sure he will agree."

Her arguments crumbled in the face of Parker's obvious confidence in her ability. "I'll call him. Please understand, that he may not want to talk to me at all." She wondered, in fact, if Ned would even accept a call from her. "I'll do my best."

Parker accepted even this limited promise with enthusiasm and they walked the perimeter of the field. Traipsing through the dirt and conversing about the project brought back a familiar sensation from the summer and Paula made a concerted effort not to let herself become too nostalgic. Fortunately, Parker kept up a constant flow of interesting, light chatter, and she allowed herself to be charmed by it. She left the site more contented than she had been in a month.

When Parker called her with an invitation to dinner a few days later, Paula accepted with anxiety.

She knew he would expect a report on her talk with Ned, and she had not yet managed to make the call. Taking her courage and self-respect in both hands, she forced herself to dial the number at the treatment facility.

Grace greeted Paula's voice with pleasure. "Oh, I'm so glad to hear from you, Paula. I had begun to think you had forgotten us out here. Ned's just gone over to another building, but I'll get him!'

"No, no, Grace. It's all right. Just let him know I called about the ethanol plant."

"Oh, I'm sure he would want me to get him, dear. He'd never forgive me if I didn't.'' And Grace put her on hold before Paula had a chance to end the conversation.

Paula drummed her fingertips on the table as she waited. Why had she agreed to this? What could she possibly hope to accomplish for Parker? What could she possibly hope to accomplish for herself? Her thoughts swirled in morbid fantasies about what Ned would say when he found out the call was from her.

"This is Andersen.'' His voice sounded so abrupt that she nearly dropped her receiver.

"Hello, Ned. This is Rosewood.'' As she spoke her courage grew, along with a certain amount of irritation.

"Oh.'' Nothing. She could scarcely believe that he would say nothing. The man must be made of ice. Paula plucked every bit of pride and anger she could find and forced it into her voice.

"I'm terribly sorry to have disturbed you. I'm calling on behalf of Parker Mills. He says he has tried several times to reach you about the sulphur dioxide problem, and that you haven't returned any of his calls. Of course, I explained that I probably wouldn't get any better hearing than he did, but that I would make the effort.''

She listened to the silence on the other end of the line, wondering what it meant. Finally, after a long minute, Ned replied. ''Look, the sulphur dioxide requires clean-up and Mills has to pay for it. You ought to know that. I thought you wanted to fight this plant, or have you finally sold out completely to the side of industry?''

Paula sucked in a sharp breath, stung terribly by the anger in his words. ''If you would just listen to what he's asking rather than being so irritable, you'd realize that I am just trying to do the job I've been paid to do. As the director of your department, you're being paid to answer his calls, so maybe you should just try to do your job. After all, if he doesn't make a go of this plant, you'll end up with a housing development out there, and I thought you said that would be even more trouble.''

''There are many things in life more troublesome than cleaning out the wastewater of a housing development!''

''Well you ought to know. Cleaning up messes and making everything sanitary seems to be your forte.''

Paula could feel her anger rising out of control, and she didn't even understand what they were arguing about. She only knew that she wanted to shout so loudly that Ned would be forced to hear her. She wanted him to . . . she wanted him to . . . She realized she wanted him to hurt as much as she did. With that realization the fight suddenly left her, and she felt more irritated with herself than with him.

Silence prevailed for a few seconds longer until Paula spoke again. ''I'm sorry. I think I'm way out of line here. I just wanted to find out if you had any suggestions that I could give to Parker.''

Ned heaved a sigh that carried through the receiver into Paula's heart. ''I'm sorry, too. I'll try to come up with something for him. I've gotten a little behind in things here, but I'll get on this right away.''

She didn't trust herself to linger because she could sense her anger ready to boil over again, so she thanked him and hung up quickly. She pledged never again to allow herself to fall in love, and she prepared to face an evening of light flirting with Parker Mills.

Parker did not flirt with her, but treated her as a respected colleague. He obviously enjoyed her company, but instead of light banter and flattery, he spoke to her with an openness and sincerity that she found immensely appealing. Unfortunately, she also found herself comparing him with Ned. In spite of the irritability of their conversation, Paula continued to feel the enticement of his attraction. She chided herself mercilessly for clinging to an impossible hope, but when Parker lightly kissed her goodnight, Paula knew they would not take the relationship any further.

Her friend and fellow teacher, Barb, having survived the rigors of teaching driver's education, badgered her about her isolation. ''Paula, you can't let one bad experience put you off men. This Parker Mills sounds like a very nice man. After all, 'a bird in the hand is worth two in the bush.' ''

Paula just shook her head and sighed. ''More clichés. I just don't feel like dating anyone else, Barb. I don't know how many chances a person has at love, but at the moment I don't think any bird in my hand is worth nearly as much as the one still sitting in the bush.''

Instead of dating, Paula tackled work with a renewed intensity, pouring every spare minute into finding creative ways to engage her students. Several times she arranged for some of her seniors to accompany her to the new site to evaluate the potential impact of the construction on the local fauna. With some feelings of subtle triumph, she noticed that the house wren population seemed to be thriving as they fattened up before their migration to their wintering grounds. Weekly phone calls with her sister and mother connected her to some awareness of family, but nothing replaced the tranquility of the brief domesticity she had shared with Ned.

One cloudless Friday in October, Paula called Sarah from school to offer her baby-sitting services for the afternoon and evening. She knew her friends rarely went out without Kevin, and she thought they could use the respite. When Paula arrived, Sarah complained that Sean hadn't returned from an inspection of the Centerville treatment facility, and Sarah had not had time even to begin to get ready. Paula took Kevin, put him in his stroller, and sent Sarah off for a long hot soak in the tub. The brilliant blue of the sky contrasted strikingly with the flashing orange and red of the maples as Paula pushed Kevin along the quiet streets of Centerville. Kevin watched solemnly each point of interest, waving arms and legs in ecstasy with the day. Once again, his beautiful innocence filled Paula with peace, and she felt her anxiety and sadness transform into hope once more.

When she finally meandered back into the Bradys' yard, Paula almost tripped over her own feet, she stopped so suddenly. Ned's car was parked in the drive. Paula nearly panicked and left again, but Kevin had begun showing signs of fatigue, and she knew she couldn't keep him out much longer. Lifting him out of the stroller, she took a deep breath and approached the door just as it opened with a slam. She saw Ned's rigid back as he spoke something into the house and she heard what sounded like "mind your own business!"

Stunned into immobility, Paula remained a few yards away from Ned, holding Kevin tightly to her chest. Ned whirled around, stalked a few feet toward his car, and froze. He looked straight at her, but for a moment Paula thought he would actually pass without speaking. He swallowed, seemed to waiver, and then took a deep breath. His ramrod straight posture became impossibly stiff, and he walked toward her.

"Hello, Paula."

Paula wondered if she would be able to force herself to speak. "H—hello, Ned." She knew her voice sounded as weak as her knees felt. She looked at him carefully, terrified by what she saw. He retained that same crisp, nearly regimental care of his clothing and his person, but in spite of that, he looked terrible. He had lost weight. His eyes bore the dark smudges of sleeplessness, and his skin appeared nearly gray from pallor. Right now he nearly sparked with anger, and Paula stepped back as if to protect Kevin.

Her movement galvanized Ned into an awareness that he had been glowering fiercely. Paula looked even more beautiful than he remembered, and he burned with frustration that he could still feel so irresistibly drawn to her. She stood there, the late afternoon sun turning her red hair into a shimmering gold, looking like some Renaissance Madonna as she held the dark-haired Kevin. Forcing himself to ignore the wrenching pain in his heart, he tried to compose his raging emotions and reassure her.

"I'm just . . . I was talking . . . I'm sorry. I'm just leaving. Please excuse me." Without another word he marched the rest of the way to his car and quickly drove away. Paula stood staring at the receding automobile, but she did not see him a few minutes later when he pulled over to the side of the road to sit perfectly immobile for ten minutes. And she didn't hear him as he shouted to himself over the pounding of his heart, "I will not do this!" By that time she had entered the Bradys' house and found Sean and Sarah standing close together watching her with concern.

"How many times do you think he had to iron those slacks to get a crease that sharp? I wish I could hire him just to do my laundry." She tried to bring it off and thought she succeeded pretty well, but they weren't fooled.

"Paula, I'm so sorry." Sean spoke into the growing silence. "I didn't expect that to happen."

"Oh no." She groaned in horror. "You weren't trying to set us up, were you?"

"No. I didn't know you were here. Ned and I had driven out together to the plant site. But when I found out you were here, I tried to get him to stay and see you. I'm sorry. He's right; it's none of my business."

Sarah spoke up angrily, "That's not true, Sean. It is your business. You're his friend and you just said you hate to see him throw away his happiness because he won't face Annie's death. Somebody has to say it to him!"

Paula knew they were being as supportive as they could, but she wished they would not interfere.

"Maybe the truth is that I'm just not the right person for Ned after all. Look, you two get ready and go out. I need to spend some serious time with my new boyfriend here. He's the most loving male in my life right now."

Hours later, Paula tried to find sleep by remembering the contentment of rocking Kevin to sleep, but the ache in her heart had been renewed, and dawn was breaking before she finally drifted off. When she awoke a short while later she had decided to take matters with Ned back into her own hands.

Chapter Nine

Hector pushed open the screen door and bounded down the steps to lunge at Paula as she opened her car door. She practically fell out of the car onto the ground as they rolled together in a playful embrace. He covered her face with his thick kisses, and she rubbed his tummy until he couldn't stand the happiness and had to run around her again.

Finally satiated, Hector rushed back up the steps to the place where Ned stood watching them. He looked as gaunt as he had the day before, but his expression held none of the hostility Paula had seen then. Instead, he looked lost. Shoving her pride to the background, she forced herself to approach him.

"Hi." She spoke with an absolutely neutral tone in spite of the turmoil in her stomach.

"Hi, yourself." So far, so good. Neither of them had said anything hurtful.

"I wondered if you would be willing to talk for

a little while," Paula asked with hardly any evidence of the tremor she felt.

Ned never moved his eyes from her face, but motioned to the porch with a tilt of his head. "Come on up."

Paula skirted around the swing with something akin to fear and chose instead to sit in one of the chairs. Ned started to sit also, then straightened and leaned back against the railing. Autumn smells drifted on the air as Paula breathed deeply to steady her nerves. Once again the beauty of the day touched her so deeply she wanted to cry out to Ned not to let this slip away from them. Instead, she sat quietly and stroked Hector's head when he placed it on her lap. She knew it fell to her to start this conversation, but for a moment she could only hold onto her precarious calm.

"I've missed you." His words startled her. So sure had she been that he would not welcome her presence that she had imagined him sitting stonily uncommunicative while she attempted to convince him to open up to her. Tears of gratitude sprang unexpectedly to her eyes.

"Thank you. I don't feel like such a total fool, knowing that." In spite of her best efforts, she knew that her anger and hurt could be heard.

"Oh, Paula, I hate myself for hurting you," he moaned, gripping the railing behind him until his knuckles turned white.

"No!" she cried. "That's a terrible kind of logic. You can't do that to me."

"What do you mean?"

"I *chose* to open my heart to you. I took the risks on my own. If you had deliberately lied to me or tried to manipulate me, you could hate yourself for that. But you can't hate yourself for not being able to love me, Ned. That's no one's fault.'' She raised her hands as if to ward off an evil presence. ''If you hate yourself for not loving me back, then I will feel responsible for you hating yourself. We can't go down that road, or we won't even be able to be friends.''

Ned started to speak, then closed his mouth and shook his head. Finally he turned away from her and looked out across the yard.

''Please, Ned. Don't shut me out of this. Whatever you feel, I want to know it.''

He faced her again and spoke very softly. ''I do love you, Paula.''

Paula's heart pounded thunderously in her chest. He loved her. What else mattered?

Ned continued speaking. ''The trouble is that it feels wrong to love you. I convinced myself that everything was all right, and then suddenly I felt as if I were having an affair. I tell myself over and over that this is stupid, that Annie is dead. . . .'' He looked at his left hand where he still wore his wedding ring. ''That Annie has been dead for a long time . . . But I still feel as if I'm cheating on her. Loving you feels like the best thing to happen to me in a long time, until it starts to feel like the worst.'' He sounded totally defeated.

Paula sat frozen. She had thought that he felt guilty because he didn't love her. How could she cope with the fact that he felt guilty because he did love her? There had to be a way through this pain. She took a deep breath and blew it out before she spoke. ''Whatever we do with this, we can't just run away from each other anymore.''

''I don't know what to do.'' He spread his hands in a gesture of futility and dropped them to his side.

''I don't either, but I know that chances for such

closeness as we've had don't come along all that often, and I'm not going to throw this one away. If it means we have to make a pact never to touch each other, then that's what I'll do.''

He shook his head. ''I don't think I can do that, Paula. I see you and I want you. It's so strong, what I feel for you. But then I torment myself with this terrible guilt.'' He looked at his wedding ring again. ''I didn't promise to love Annie until she died. I promised to love her forever.''

''Ned Andersen, you listen to me. I don't want to make you stop loving Annie. I think I would have liked her if I had ever known her. But I won't accept that you and I can't be friends. Even if Annie was alive, we could be friends!''

Her passionate speech brought her to her feet and raised the color in her cheeks. She stretched to her full height of five feet, and she clenched her fists in frustration. Ned watched this tiny warrior prepare to do battle, and he couldn't help himself. He started to laugh.

''Oh, Paula. You are wonderful. I don't know if I'm strong enough to keep up with you, but I do agree that we have to try. I never laugh when you're not around. I can't stand the thought of not having you as my friend.''

Suddenly Paula laughed, too, the contagion of his change in spirits infecting her with a delightful relief. She stuck her hand out and he shook it. ''Friends,'' she stated emphatically.

''Friends.''

Of course, they remained awkward with each other. Hector provided a perfect buffer, receiving more affection than ever when either Paula or Ned needed to touch. Instead of the familiar, easy reaching out for a hand or cheek, they held themselves carefully apart, usually with Hector between them.

They spent the afternoon working around the house, cleaning out gutters and spreading mulch for the winter. Paula had brought a present of several bird feeders, which she placed around the property for use as the harvest waned and the weather grew colder. Ned worried that Paula would feel cheated, spending her day off doing work for his house, until she promised to collect her reward by making him help her put together a teaching unit on water management.

By early evening—they were tired and hungry, and Ned suggested they go out for dinner.

"No," Paula insisted. "We can eat here if you want, or I can just get something at home. I don't want to start 'sneaking around' again." They were standing in the living room and Paula walked to the mantel. Picking up Annie's portrait, she studied the beautiful smile and similar coloring. "I don't want to be Annie's enemy, Ned."

She could see that he struggled with the sight of her holding the picture, but he didn't leave or become angry. He finally simply shrugged his shoulders and said, "I'll start some chicken."

Gradually, over the next few months, they developed a pattern of coping with the tension between them. When together, they would keep busy with some task requiring hard work, and they spent most of their time either outside or with friends. Ned apologized to Sean for losing his temper, and that friendship continued as strong as ever. In fact, only Sean and Sarah understood the nature of Ned and Paula's friendship. To other outsiders, their relationship probably looked like a typical romance, but to Paula and Ned, the strictures against anything romantic held firm.

When Paula put a platform feeder outside her apartment window, she also took several feeders to the Preston water treatment facility office to place around the grounds. There she learned how Ned's coworkers viewed her relationship with him.

Ned's secretary, Grace, greeted Paula like a long-lost friend. "Oh I am so glad that you two have settled your differences. Ned's a different person when you're around. Of course he's always the perfect gentleman to me, but I just mean he's happier when he has you around. You know what I mean."

Paula had accepted the compliment as a social nicety rather than as a true insight, until two other of Ned's subordinates made almost identical comments. She finally accepted the fact that their friendship probably benefitted him as much as it did her. As long as they could avoid too much strain from their self-imposed prohibition on touching, they thrived in each other's company as good friends. Sometimes, even Paula felt as if Annie accompanied them and had simply stepped out of sight for the moment.

With Paula's encouragement, Ned talked about Annie and their life together, realizing that he had hardly been able to mention her since her death. By remembering the earlier years of his marriage, Ned slowly began to heal some of his enormous wound; and at times he almost managed to pretend that Paula was simply a friend of the family. At other times, the platonic nature of their relationship nearly resulted in a massive explosion.

As the weather grew colder and the school year progressed, Paula normally spent her time with study or paperwork. One evening, Barbara had joined them for dinner at Paula's apartment, and the three had laughed for a couple of hours over various high school antics of Barbara's and Paula's students. Barbara left early to grade papers, and they settled down for a quiet evening, Ned reading and Paula preparing a new study guide for her first semester final. Mozart played softly in the background, and they worked companionably for another hour.

Taking a break, Ned prepared them some tea and brought it back to the table where Paula worked. He set the mugs down and leaned over her shoulder to see what she had done. "This is very nice," he commented, reaching over her to point to her diagram of a bright green *Euglena* and placing his other hand on her shoulder. "I didn't realize that you're an artist."

"I'm not. One of my students did that for me," she laughed, turning to face him. He remained bent close to her with his hand on the table and looked into her laughing eyes. Her nearness affected him like a charge of electricity, and he remained paralyzed, unwilling to give in to his desire but unable to retreat.

Paula, too, knew she was trapped in the intensity of attraction between them but felt helpless to move one way or the other. She watched him swallow and her own mouth felt dry. The fragile balance of their compromise teetered precariously and she felt panic rising as Ned slowly moved closer to her. If he kissed her, he would feel compelled to break off the friendship. Paula knew that to be true even though he had never made the rules so clear.

"Where's Hector when we need him?" She heard her voice, high and tight with her attempt to break the spell.

It worked. Ned backed quickly away and looked around the room as if actually searching for the dog.

His breathing came in short puffs as if he were exhausted from a sprint, and he squinted in consternation. "I think maybe I'd better be getting home," he rasped at last.

Paula remained seated until Ned had donned his coat and reached the door. "Ned," she called as he put his hand on the knob. He turned back toward her. "We'll know better next time," she reassured him. With a brief nod, he walked out.

Paula raged at herself, at Ned, and finally at Annie, but eventually calmed down enough to remember that she had made this bargain with her eyes wide open. Ned had made no vague promises about the future; he had promised to remain faithful to his wife. Paula wondered if she was deceiving herself with the hope that somehow Ned would eventually resolve his grief and be able to love again. After that evening, they carefully spent quiet evenings with Hector as chaperone, and they scrupulously avoided contact.

What worked best for them were those times when Ned joined Paula and Barbara with their students at the preserve. A flock of Canada geese typically wintered at the Hadley Reservoir, and Paula encouraged her students to keep records of their numbers. She wondered if the construction would affect the birds that depended so heavily on field corn leftovers. Happily tramping through other nearby fields, the students and their adult guides found ample evidence that the wintering birds would have plenty to eat. Ned revealed a natural gift for teaching, and Barb repeatedly congratulated Paula on her good fortune.

"It's a good idea to bring him along with the students, Paula. That way you can get a realistic idea of how he is with children. You know, 'never buy a pig in a poke.' "

Paula almost choked at that. ''Barbara, just how many quaint little adages do you know?''

''At least a million.''

''Well, try to remember 'all that glitters isn't gold,' '' Paula retorted, leaving Barbara wondering what she might have missed seeing in this man who seemed so perfect for her friend.

For Christmas vacation Paula decided to fly back to Savannah. Her mother's osteoporosis had become so severe that she could not walk without assistance. Paula's sister visited the nursing home daily to provide their mother with more exercise than the staff alone could provide. Paula had wanted her mother to come to Ohio, but Ruth Rosewood hated the cold winters and insisted on remaining in Savannah. Now she could no longer travel at all, and Joan bore her filial duties without much of a break. Finally, Paula convinced her sister and brother-in-law to take a vacation and let Paula remain to help Ruth.

''Oh, Mama, I've missed you so much.'' Paula leaned down to gently hug the tiny figure in the wheelchair. To her dismay, her mother winced at the light pressure, and Paula immediately released her. ''Are you in much pain?''

Ruth rolled her eyes. ''Much pain, she asks! Honestly, Paula, what do you expect? Of course I'm in pain. The world is full of crime, there are drug dealers in the grade schools, the oceans are being polluted, and Johnny Carson retired. Who wouldn't be in much pain?''

''Oh, Mama, you're too much.'' Paula marveled at her mother's ability to joke even in the face of the dreadful disease. ''I want to be just like you.''

Their reunion filled Paula with jumbled emotions: pleasure with her mother's humor, anxiety about her mother's condition, and an awareness that not much longer would she have her mother's sheltering love. With assistance from the nursing home staff, Paula arranged to take her mother to the shore for a while. Sitting in her wheelchair on the boardwalk, Ruth breathed deeply of the salt air and laughed at the sassing gulls.

"This is what it's all about, Paula."

"What, Mama? Seagulls?"

"Yes, Miss Smarty, seagulls, and the ocean, and this planet so full of life. Here we are, and we should love and cherish every minute we have to experience it."

Paula watched as her mother tossed bread crumbs at the vigilant gulls, who immediately called in the rest of their kind until Paula thought they were in the midst of a remake of Hitchcock's film *The Birds*. Eventually, the birds realized that the food was gone, and they abandoned their patroness in search of another; but Paula thought she would never forget the image of her tiny mother sitting in her wheelchair surrounded by hundreds of fluttering white wings like a band of angels carrying off her chariot.

To her surprise, Paula received several long telephone calls from Ned while she stayed at her sister's home. He knew the ravages of watching a loved one live with constant pain, and he listened to Paula's worries with a deep understanding. He never hesitated to ask about her concerns, and by sharing some of her own feelings of helplessness, she opened a new door for him. In his efforts to empathize with her grief he finally began expressing some of his own.

Near the end of her stay she revealed her worst fear. "Today was so terrible for her, Ned. She cried and cried, she hurt so much. When I tried to help her, I only made it worse. Finally she asked me to leave. She said my worry only made her feel guilty, and that she wished she would die and relieve us all of the burden of taking care of her."

"I'm so sorry, Paula."

"The worst of it is that a part of me . . . I don't know how to say this. . . . I know she would be happier . . . I don't know. I just don't want her to suffer any more." Paula's voice had become so soft, Ned could barely hear her.

He sat silently, hundreds of miles away from her, but knowing exactly how devastating it was to find oneself in that place. "I understand, Paula. I . . . I . . ." His voice broke as he remembered sitting for hours watching Annie battle valiantly with her pain. Wanting to pray that she would die soon, so it would all be over, and not able to pray for such a thing. Not able to admit feeling such a thing. Still not able to admit the relief he had felt when her suffering finally ended.

"Ned? Are you still there?"

"I know how you feel. I felt the same way about . . . Annie." Shame flooded him even as he spoke the words. How could he live with himself after such an admission?

"Thanks, Ned. One of the nurses here told me it's a normal feeling, but knowing you've been there helps me not hate myself so much."

What had she said? Ned knew this was important, but he couldn't cope with the rush of emotions engulfing him. Everything Paula had said had brought back times he had agonized over Annie's suffering. He had ruthlessly ignored his own reactions, refusing to acknowledge that he was also being ravaged by the cancer. He dealt with his grief the same way he dealt with all difficulties. He simply worked harder, more deliberately, more precisely, and less emotionally. There had been times when he thought he had destroyed his ability to feel anything at all.

Then Paula had entered his life and he learned that the feelings weren't destroyed but simply hiding, waiting for the chance to slip past his defenses and devastate him. Losing her had nearly killed him because of the effort it took to keep the pain at bay. Now things were easier, most of the time. He could almost convince himself that Annie still sat just out of sight. Having Paula's friendship made it easier because he could keep busy and actually enjoy himself sometimes. But these moments of revelation kept hitting him, moments like now when he felt the touch of all those hidden feelings. And of course, there were the other moments, the moments when he knew he loved Paula so very deeply, and he ran headlong into a wall of guilt.

Paula stopped talking. She knew Ned had gone away somewhere and couldn't hear her. More and more, that seemed to happen, and she could only wait until he had dealt with his personal demons and returned to her.

Finally he spoke into the silence. "I'm sorry, Paula. I guess I got distracted."

"That's okay. I'll see you when I get home."

"I don't want to let you down, Paula. I . . . know you need someone to listen to this. I do know how hard it is. I do understand."

"I know you do, Ned. And it really helps."

When Paula went to say good-bye to her mother, the next day, Ruth appeared to be in less pain than she had been since Paula's arrival. "See, they can't keep a good woman down," she exclaimed. However, they spent the time together with Ruth remaining in bed. Paula asked the nurse, and discovered that Ruth's physician had increased her pain medication, but Ruth didn't want to talk about that.

"Paula, I know what's in store for me. It's what's in store for you that has me worried."

"What do you mean, Mama?"

"I know you'll be all right after I'm gone. You're a good girl, a smart girl. You'll be fine. But I don't want you to lose out on your life because you're stuck on this fella who can't get over his wife."

"Mama! You're the one who told me not to give up if I love him."

"I'm the one who told you to figure out what the right thing was, and not to run away. I wonder now if maybe by going back and putting up with his problem, you're letting him run away."

"You're confusing me."

Ruth patted her daughter's hand in the familiar way Paula loved so much. "Don't make it too easy for him to escape what he needs to do, Paula. When I die, you are going to have to grieve. I wish you didn't have to, but you will. Just the way I grieved when my mother died. Just the way we all grieved when your father died. You know what it is like. We hated feeling so sad, but eventually the sadness goes away."

Paula nodded, remembering the times the three Rosewood women had bolstered each other through the terrible loss of John. "Don't you think I can help Ned do that?"

Ruth shrugged. "I know you can help. I don't know if your Ned will let you."

Recognizing the truth in her mother's wise words, Paula nodded again. "What would I ever do without you, Mama?"

Ruth laughed. "You would come to visit your sister and leave with a suntan instead of that pale white stuff you have from spending your vacation inside!"

Paula laughed, too. "Mama, even without you, this freckled skin of mine will never tan."

She attached a bird feeder to the window ledge of her mother's room and provided a huge bag of bird-seed for the staff to put out. "When the house wrens leave Ohio, sometimes they winter in Georgia, Mama. I want you to think of me when they come to visit you here."

"Why do you think they will come here?"

"They always know a good home when they see one."

Paula left soon after to return to the bleak Ohio winter, semester finals, and an excited Parker Mills, but not to Ned Andersen.

Chapter Ten

Paula jammed her master copy of the first semester's final exam into her desk drawer and locked it. Outside the classroom window total darkness greeted her martyred sigh. No matter how hard she pushed herself, she could never manage to complete all her work and still leave this building before dark during the long miserable months of winter. When she emerged from the building a few minutes later, the sting of cold winter rain only increased her irritability. What a way to spend her first day back from the warm, gentle Georgia climate.

"It's only the winter blues," she argued with herself. "Go home and drink some hot chocolate."

By the time she had peeled off her wet clothes, wrapped herself in her favorite terry cloth bathrobe, and started some hot water, Paula had convinced herself that she felt fine. Her answering machine blinked insistently at her, and she played the tape back as she poured her hot chocolate.

"Paula! How was your flight back? Would you like to get some dinner? Call me at home."

Ned's familiar voice sounded vibrant, enthusiastic. Paula's heart responded with the customary flutter of welcome, and she reached for the phone, but her mother's words came back to her. *Don't make it too easy for him to escape what he needs to do.*

Did she make it too easy for Ned? Was she so desperate for his companionship that she had been willing to sacrifice love in order to spend time with him? Did her willingness to accept second best allow him to avoid resolving Annie's death? Paula hadn't wanted to interfere with Ned's choice. She had believed that he would handle his feelings in time, but perhaps her mother was right. Perhaps she had made it too easy for him, and the resulting restrictions on their relationship hurt them both.

Slowly she withdrew her hand from the telephone. They had not seen each other for nearly three weeks now. If she called him, they would be right back where they had been before: afraid to get too close, afraid to touch each other, living like friends but all the while feeling the terrible tension of repressed love. She knew she couldn't continue to spend time with him, denying the true feelings in her heart. Her escape last summer may have been precipitous, but she knew now that her flight had been the only way.

In spite of her resolution, she had allowed herself to become involved with a married man; no matter that the relationship appeared to be platonic, no matter that the man's wife had been dead for five years. She had given him her entire heart, but he was not free to return her love. Now she had only one course of action left. She would stop seeing him.

Paula huddled in the corner of her sofa, sipping the hot chocolate, and repeating her resolution over and over to herself. If she exerted enough will power, she could keep her resolution; however, she would not depend on herself alone. Picking up the phone, she began calling friends and arranging enough activities to keep her busy for the next week.

Over the next several days Ned called repeatedly, each time sounding more concerned and confused. Paula could hear the hurt in his voice, and she argued endlessly with herself that she at least owed him an explanation of her actions; but she feared her own weakness, knowing that if he asked her to reconsider, she would lose her resolution. She stopped answering when the phone rang in case it was Ned, but she forced herself to listen to his messages, as if in penance for the pain she knew she was causing him.

"Paula. It's me again. . . . I wish you would pick up the phone. . . . I know you must be angry about something. . . . Well I don't know it, but I guess you must be. . . . I . . . Please talk to me, Paula. . . . I want—I know I let you down that last time we talked. . . . I'm sorry. . . . I—call me. . . . Please."

The message had been sent early that morning, before the time she normally left for school. The futility of his request sounded in every word, and Paula thought she couldn't bear this any longer. He was blaming himself for the wrong thing. She reached for the instrument to call him when its piercing bell jolted her back in surprise. She determined to answer this time. Whatever happened, she couldn't avoid him any longer.

"Paula!" Parker Mills's excited voice came unexpectedly through the receiver. "Are you busy?

I've got the greatest news! Come to dinner with me and we'll celebrate!''

''What is it?''

''No. I'll tell you when I get there. Half an hour?''

''Fine,'' Paula answered, wondering if this interruption was a sign that she shouldn't return Ned's call. ''I'll be ready.''

With some difficulty, she dressed to go out. Every few minutes she would return to the telephone as if she would just try to reach him for a few minutes, but shaking her head, she would walk away and resume brushing her hair, putting on her shoes, perfecting her lipstick. Finally she had no more distractions, yet Parker would not arrive for at least ten minutes. Paula sat in the living room and stared at the telephone, wishing she could make sense of the mess of her life.

''If I call him now, I won't be able to talk for long anyway. Maybe that's the best thing to do.'' She lifted the receiver and dialed Ned's home, waiting through ring after ring. ''Okay, he's not there. Does that mean I'm off the hook, or does that mean this is a test of my determination to do the right thing?'' In frustration she ran both hands through her hair, destroying immediately the sleek effect she had managed to create. She lifted the receiver again, this time dialing the number at the water treatment facility office.

''Sorry, Paula.'' Grace spoke with real regret. ''To tell you the truth, I don't think anybody here has seen him all day. He said something yesterday about checking out some leaks in a line west of Centerville, but I didn't think he would be there all day. Maybe he ran into more trouble than he expected.'' She paused before adding hesitantly, ''Do you want me to give him a message? I know he's been trying to reach you. I'm getting ready to leave here, but I can put a message on his desk.''

Instantly contrite, Paula understood how much her refusal to speak with Ned would have worried his friends at the plant. They adhered loyally to the belief that he could do no wrong, except perhaps when assigning weekend emergency duty, and all of them had graciously informed Paula that she had been good for him. If he suffered now, they must surely have felt the impact.

''Sure, Grace,'' Paula acquiesced. ''Let him know I called and that I'll try again tomorrow.'' Her conscience appeased, Paula waited for Parker's knock and the distraction of his good news.

Dinner proved to be even more than a distraction, Parker really celebrated some exciting news. The Ontario Corn Producers Association, in conjunction with the U.S. Department of Energy, had granted several large research awards for ethanol production research. Based on the work Paula had begun during the summer, Parker had written a proposal to evaluate the economic feasibility of combining ethanol production with wastewater treatment. Already a number of water treatment plants produced methane, but the required scrubbing process reduced the profitability of the ventures. Now Parker sought to find a different relationship, with ethanol fueling the pumps and aerators, and the sludge fertilizing the cornfields. The cleaned water could be used in the soaking tubs without the added fluoride and chlorine of drinking water, and then could be filtered and sent on to the river or drinking water treatment facilities.

''They've approved the research proposal, and we'll even be able to include an ongoing study of the ecosystem of the plant site, Paula. I hope you'll accept the job of coordinating that project.''

"I'm truly impressed, Parker. I had no idea that you even intended to apply for a research grant."

"Actually . . ." He grinned a little sheepishly. "It was Ned's idea. He never ceases to amaze me, the way he finds connections between everything."

Paula thought about how much she missed that ability of Ned's to make connections. He added so much to her own ability to understand the environment, as if the two of them together created a synergy that enhanced their individual talents.

"By the way," Parker continued. "I never did thank you for making that phone call to Ned last fall. Without that, I wouldn't have had a prayer. Ned had heard some good news from fellow water experts in Nebraska about a new dry grind method. It's a new procedure for separating the germ from the fermentable mass before the milling procedure. I'll be able to use the germ, which does not ferment to ethanol, to produce corn oil."

"That should increase your profit margin some!"

"Better yet, the dry grind method allows us to soak the corn in plain water instead of in sulphur dioxide. The runoff will be very clean because the fermentation process uses nearly everything except the germ used to produce the corn oil. The water can be sent directly to the wetland area!"

Once again Paula's thoughts drifted back to Ned, remembering how angry they had been during that telephone conversation. She marveled that he had even remembered the point of her call, much less acted on it.

"Paula?" Parker looked at her with a grin. "So, will you take it?"

"What?" She had lost the thread of the conversation.

"Will you take the position? Will you coordinate the ecology study?"

"Parker, I'd love to. I assume I could work it around my teaching schedule. Could I use some of my students to collect data? They would learn so much!"

"Aha! You're already doing the job. I knew you'd want it. This is the most optimistic I've felt since I first bought that property. We'll find an economic way to produce renewable fuels yet."

With enthusiasm they spent another two hours discussing the possibilities for both studies, and Paula managed to banish her depressing thoughts about Ned. As they left the restaurant, Paula saw with some gratitude that the temperature had finally dropped enough to change the rain to snow. The white covering reflected the few Preston streetlights and brightened the scene. Paula felt her spirits lift accordingly, and she sincerely thanked Parker for including her in his celebration.

"I thought Ned would be able to join us, but I couldn't reach him all day. Is he working late?" Parker presumed her response and continued. "Will you let him know the good news when you see him?" His trust that Paula would know Ned's whereabouts reminded her of how much her friends assumed about her relationship with Ned.

"Sure, Parker," she replied with a small sigh. "I'll let him know when I talk to him."

Filled with contradictory feelings, Paula returned to her apartment. She wanted to talk with Ned so desperately that she felt her muscles tensing in an effort to run to the phone, but she feared hearing his voice again, knowing that nothing would have changed between them. *How long am I going to go on torturing myself over this man?* she wondered with exasperation as she noticed the blinking light on her answering machine. In surrender she pressed the key to play the message.

"Paula . . ." Hector's whine in the background nearly drowned out the whisper that was Ned's voice. "Paula, I need . . . your . . . help." More whining and then barking. The receiver crashed against something, probably the side of the phone, and then came a thundering crash as something heavy fell against the table that held the phone. A few more sounds of the receiver being banged against something were followed by the click of the connection being broken.

Paula stared at her machine as if it had become some alien piece of technology she had never seen before. What on earth had that been about? Suddenly all of her soul-searching appeared ridiculous. Ned needed help. He had sounded as if he were hurt or ill. Nothing else mattered but that she get to him as quickly as possible.

She dialed his number and listened to the repeated unanswered ringing. "Come on, Ned. Where are you?" Finally she hung up in frustration. Grabbing her coat and keys she raced down the stairs to her car. The rain had frozen to a sheet of sheer ice beneath the light covering of snow, and Paula slid most of the way through the parking lot only to find the car door frozen shut. With a burst of angry energy, she kicked it hard with her booted foot, jarring the ice loose, and grabbed the handle with both hands. When she pulled with her full strength, the door flew open, knocking her to the ground.

Paula was in no mood to worry about the jolt to her shoulder, and she jumped in behind the wheel. Fortunately one result of last summer's tornado had been her purchase of a reliable vehicle, and the engine started immediately. She roared out of the parking lot, spinning into a skid as she hit the street. *Be careful,* she admonished herself. *Don't be stupid. You can't help him if you're in a ditch.* She kept up the diatribe, managing to hold her speed to dangerous rather than suicidal.

She approached each landmark on the way to his home with agonizing slowness, all the time fighting with fantasies about what could be wrong. Finally she saw the turnoff up the sheltered drive to his home, and she pulled in beside his car. No lights shone through the drawn curtains, and there was no indication of any problem. Perhaps he had simply unplugged the phone and gone to bed. What was she doing here? She wondered at her own panic. Perhaps she should just turn around and go back home.

Unable to leave without allaying her fears, Paula stepped out of the car and listened. Hector's unmistakable sounds of distress suddenly broke loose from the house. He was barking loudly, scratching frantically at the door. She saw his head push through the curtains at the dark living-room window, and he barked furiously when he saw her.

Surely Ned would come to quiet the dog; he never allowed Hector to behave this way. But the house remained dark and quiet except for Hector's insistent noise. Paula made her decision and ran up the steps. The movement caused a sharp pain in her shoulder, but she ignored it. Using her other arm she began pounding on the door and calling Ned's name. The longer she remained there, the worse her fears became, and finally she began searching through her cache of keys to find the one that would open this door.

At last she had the door open. Hector jumped to her face, then retreated across the room, barking continuously in spite of the fact that he had started to lose sound. "It's all right, Hector. Calm down. Where's Ned?" Paula reached for the lamp on one of the end tables and tripped over Ned's leg where it extended beyond the couch. She fell in a heap, crying out with the excruciating pain that gripped her right shoulder and arm as she tried to catch herself.

Ned lay beside her, unmoved by her fall or her cry, oblivious to anything, and for a moment Paula experienced the terror of thinking he was dead. Then Hector finally stopped barking, and in the silence she could hear Ned's ragged breathing. She touched his face. It burned so hotly she jerked her hand away.

"Ned? Can you hear me?" Echoes of his rescue of her last summer teased at her consciousness briefly, but she shoved them away ruthlessly as she centered all of her thoughts on saving this man she loved so much.

Chapter Eleven

Paula slumped against the orange vinyl cushions of the three-seater in the ICU waiting room. Her head had begun throbbing with a dull ache, and she wanted to close her eyes against the painkiller-induced nausea. At least the sharp agony in her shoulder had disappeared after the clinic doctor had insisted on wrapping it and giving her a sling for her arm. "Not dislocated, but a severe sprain," he'd said. She called herself seven different kinds of fool for the injury, but at least receiving her own treatment had kept her occupied while Ned was in surgery.

She had been in to see him twice since the operation, stroking his arm and speaking softly until she realized the nurse was watching her.

"It's okay, honey," the woman had reassured her. "It helps them if you talk to them. He needs to know you're here."

And so, for ten minutes out of every hour she was allowed to enter the tiny cubicle where Ned lay, pale under his normal windburn, with tubes leading into and out of his body. He looked so fragile as he lay there that Paula wondered where her Ned had gone. Where was that caustic wit and that rigid emotional control? She couldn't find it in this creature whose breathing and heart rate were being drawn on graphs beside his narrow bed.

Now she looked at the large wall clock, counting down until she could see him again, trying not to castigate herself any more for the perversity of her nature that had kept her from him the only time he had ever admitted needing her.

"Ms. Rosewood?" A tall scrub-suited man glanced around at the residents of the waiting room, searching for some sign of acknowledgment from the owner of the name. Paula started to rise, only to collapse back against the chair with a grunt when she lost her balance. Gritting her teeth against the strain to her shoulder, she braced her feet beneath the sinking chair and pushed herself up; the doctor managed to reach her in time to ineffectually place a hand beneath her good elbow.

"I'm Dr. Levinthal. Please come with me," he commanded with a subdued authority that spoke of serious concerns and absolute certainty of obedience.

Paula would have gone with him to Hades if it meant she could learn something about Ned, and she followed him to a small office just inside the closed ICU doors.

"You're related to Mr. Andersen?" he asked, leaning against the metal desk crowded into the office.

"No, just a friend."

His eyes drifted to a small sign posted above the

nurse's station, which proclaimed that only immediate family were allowed the ten-minute visitations.
Paula rolled her own eyes in exasperation and said
impulsively, "I'm the closest thing he's had to family since his wife died."

He raised one eyebrow, picked up a paper clip and
rotated it between his fingers for a few minutes.
"The nurse said you called the squad and came in
with him."

Paula's head had begun to hurt again, and she
found she had no patience to wait while this man
decided whether or not to tell her anything. "Look.
Ned and I are very good friends. He called me, apparently right after he started becoming ill, but I was
out for the evening. As soon as I got the message, I
went to his home. I found him already unconscious
and I called the squad. I intend to stay here until I
know he's all right and I can talk to him. Could you
please just tell me what happened?" She had begun
trembling about halfway through the story, and in
spite of her best efforts to be strong, she had tears
in her eyes by the time she finished.

Dr. Levinthal nodded once as if in decision. "His
appendix ruptured and we're concerned about peritonitis. He hemorrhaged pretty seriously, and quite
frankly, it's still touch-and-go. He isn't coming out
of the anesthesia the way I want. . . . I've seen this
before with very ill people who don't particularly
want to get well. They can just slip away."

Paula felt her world fall apart. Was this the choice
Ned wanted to make? He had always seemed to love
life so much. Even in the moments of sadness, he
hadn't wanted to give up.

Levinthal continued talking. "I would like to ask
you to stay with him for a while if you don't mind.

If you could talk to him, let him know you're there, he might respond.''

Paula grabbed a tissue from the desk and grumbled, ''That's what I've been trying to get someone to let me do all night. Of course I'll stay with him.'' She walked to the door and then returned to the desk. ''I need to make a phone call first.''

Daylight was lightening the windows, and Paula reached Barb who had just begun preparing for school. Paula had accumulated plenty of sick leave, and the sprained shoulder provided enough excuse for her to justify taking time off without explaining why she needed to be absent for someone not in her immediate family. With her lesson plans prepared well in advance, Paula knew she could afford to let a substitute teach her classes for several days, but she asked Barb to keep an eye out for her students, just in case any problems arose.

''I hate not being there for them, Barb, but I don't know how I can leave Ned right now. I don't think I could keep my mind on teaching, knowing that he is here needing me.'' Paula tried to keep her voice calm and detached, but she choked at the thought of Ned's pale, still body lying in the cubicle across from the nurses' station.

''Paula, go on. I'll take care of everything. I'll even call Mr. Reinhardt for you. Should I call anyone else?''

''Call Grace, out at the treatment plant. She'll know how to reach Ned's family. None of them live in Ohio, but I think they'd want to know about this right away. And could you call my friend Sarah? She and Sean will need to get Hector.''

''Got it. Now don't worry about anything else but helping Ned get well.''

As she hung up the phone, Paula felt her knees

go weak with the fear that nothing she did could be enough to help Ned overcome this. She hurried across the corridor to his side, once again listening to the muted beeping of his monitors and observing each rise of his chest with his shallow, rasping breaths. He looked so frail, his eyelashes nearly invisible in the dark smudges beneath his eyes, his sunken cheeks ashen from loss of blood.

"Ned, please come back," she whispered as she took his left hand in both of hers. She looked at the place where his ring had been removed, noticing the small white band in an otherwise brown and roughened hand. "Please don't give up."

One of the nurses came quietly to her side, carrying a plastic and steel desk chair, the kind she most hated from the long tables in the school library. Some sadistic entrepreneur had invented these chairs, whose sole desirable characteristic was their ability to be stacked upon each other twelve high. "It's not very comfortable, but it's probably better than standing," she murmured sympathetically to Paula. "Would you like some coffee?"

Paula felt such gratitude that she couldn't speak and merely nodded her head. She talked on and on to Ned, sometimes imagining that he moved an eyebrow in response, sometimes convinced that he had stopped breathing altogether. She talked about Hector, how frantic he had been when the rescue squad had taken Ned away on the stretcher last night; she told him about her mother, how much Ned's conversations had helped when Paula was in Georgia. She told him about Parker Mills's grant, and how grateful Parker was for Ned's insights.

Sometime after her second cup of coffee, Paula began talking to Annie, instead of to Ned. She felt as if she were doing battle for his soul, even though a part of her brain remained rational enough to chastise herself for being ridiculous.

"Let him go, Annie. He has the right to live. Please let him go." Over and over she repeated her plea. "Let him go. Let him go." She laid her aching head against the mattress, kissed his hand, and held it to her cheek. *Let him go,* she thought as she finally succumbed to the pull of exhaustion, medication, and dread and fell into an uneasy sleep.

Fingers pulled through her tangled hair with a familiar tug, then stroked her cheek and lips. Paula opened her eyes to see Ned's hand moving once more to touch her head. She grabbed his fingers and sat up straight to look into his eyes.

"I thought I had lost you." They both spoke the words at the same time.

"Oh, Ned." Paula's heart pounded thunderously as if awakening so suddenly had sent a surge of adrenaline pumping through her veins.

"I thought I would never see you again." The hoarseness of his voice reminded her of her duty, and she reached up to press the call button at the head of his bed. Ned retrieved her hand and brought her fingertips to his lips. "I thought I would never see you again," he repeated.

Paula couldn't speak. The only thing she could imagine doing was leaning down and kissing him, but in spite of the tenderness of his words, she knew the taboo still withheld her. Ned pulled slightly on her hand, drawing her closer to him. "Paula..."

"Mr. Andersen, you're finally awake! How wonderful!" The nurse pushed around to the other side of the bed, checking on the IV and the drainage tubes. With a practiced movement she opened a plastic thermometer strip and said, "Open up, please. Sorry about this, but we need to check your temperature carefully. We don't want to take any chances with infection.'' She chattered incessantly while she worked, and Paula noticed Ned's eyes glaze over and begin to close before the nurse had even completed her chores.

''He's fallen asleep again,'' Paula moaned. ''Is he all right?''

''Don't worry,'' the nurse reassured her. ''He'll be in and out for the rest of the day, but now he seems to be progressing.'' She jotted vital sign information on the chart hanging on the end of Ned's bed, patted Paula on the shoulder, and moved on to another patient.

Managing only a few brief escapes to the ladies room, Paula remained by Ned's side until late in the evening. Each time he awoke, she greeted his return with more optimism, and by evening he managed to remain awake long enough to speak with her for more than a few minutes.

''You must have gotten my phone message.'' He smiled crookedly.

''Actually, I tried to call you before that last message, but you weren't home.''

''That was you calling? I was home, but I felt too sick to move. I'm not sure how I managed to get to the phone for that last call. I just knew I needed you.''

Once more, he reached for her hand, and she extended her fingers to his willingly. This time as he pulled her toward him, she felt her resistance melting, and she knew she was about to step over that boundary of safety they had so firmly established between themselves. This time the interruption came from the physician, not the nurse.

''Are you still here, Ms. Rosewood?'' Dr. Levinthal asked as he strode into the room. ''I think

Mr. Andersen can survive without your ministrations for a few hours." In fact, Ned had improved enough that the surgeon agreed to move him from the ICU to a general medical floor in the morning.

"Ms. Rosewood, you should go home now," Dr. Levinthal suggested. "Mr. Andersen will likely sleep the entire night, and you've had a rough day. How's your shoulder?"

"What happened to your shoulder?" Ned asked, still clinging to her hand, as he had done each time he awoke.

"I slipped on the ice last night, like the klutz I am." Paula laughed. "I just didn't want you to get all the attention."

"Sounds about right," he muttered sleepily, with a slight smile on his face. "You need someone to watch out for you."

Paula felt a slight pressure as he squeezed her fingers and she laughed. "Yeah, right. Someone big and strong like you. Someone who doesn't know enough to go to the doctor when he's sick."

Ned mumbled something she couldn't hear.

"What was that, Ned?"

"I said maybe you're not the only one who needs someone to watch out for them." He closed his eyes as if to avoid her next comment and within minutes he had drifted off again. Dr. Levinthal steered Paula out of the room.

"Goodnight, Ms. Rosewood. Go home now."

Paula thought the idea of going home was an excellent one, but she didn't believe she could actually manage to walk all the way to the elevator, much less drive all the way home. Fortunately, when she still faced half the distance to the elevator, its doors opened and out came Sarah and Sean Brady. They gathered her in, listened to her report on Ned's condition, and finally bundled her into their car.

She remembered nothing more until she awoke the next morning to the smell of coffee and oatmeal, the sounds of the Brady family preparing for breakfast, and the feel of Hector's cold nose pressed firmly against her ear.

"Hey there, boy, how ya doin'?" she mumbled into his fur as she wrapped his comforting warmth around her. "Your boss is going to be okay, Hector. Don't you worry."

Sarah entered the room with Kevin on her hip and a cup of coffee in her other hand. "Good morning! I thought Hector would be more polite than to wake you up, but I think he couldn't wait to see you."

"He's better than any alarm clock I ever met." Paula yawned as she accepted the coffee. "Have you heard anything from the hospital?"

"No news is good news, Paula. I'm sure you can take a little break before you go back. You looked like death itself last night."

"No news is good news. There really is a platitude for every possible life situation, isn't there?" Paula laughed ruefully. But knowing that Sarah's advice made good sense, Paula took time to eat before Sarah drove her home to clean up.

Snow-covered fields reflected the brilliant winter sun. Passing the preserve on the way into Preston, Paula stared at the bird boxes scattered tall and empty across the stark fields. Construction machinery remained stationary on the frozen land beyond the preserve, but even in this weather, workers already gathered to begin the process of creating the new plant. If she had her students out there right now, she would be showing them how alive the system was even in the dead of winter. Only a few days remained in January, and by February she would be able to show them evidence of new growth on some plants. Now only the nonmigratory birds huddled in fluffed up balls of insulating feathers. But by March, the Centerville bald eagles would return to begin adding on to their nests, and the house wrens would begin their compulsive building. All of nature conspired to remind Paula that the dormancy of winter only served as a temporary cover to the natural progression of life toward growth and reproduction.

Paula stirred uneasily in the passenger seat and Sarah cast a worried glance in her direction. "How is your shoulder, Paula?"

"It's sore, that's all."

"Is everything else all right?"

"I wish I knew, Sarah. I can't bother about the future until I know that Ned is going to be all right." She opened her mouth to continue, but then stopped and simply shook her head.

Sarah reached over and squeezed her friend's hand in silent understanding.

When they finally reached the hospital, they learned that Ned had already been moved to his new room and was in good condition. They found his door open and a woman carrying a large floral arrangement standing at the foot of his bed. She laughed as she placed the flowers on a table and walked around the bed to kiss Ned on the forehead.

Paula started to back out of the room, but Sarah pushed her in, saying as she entered, "So, Ned, you'll do anything to have a roomful of women paying attention to you."

"Sarah! Paula!" His smile lit up his face, which continued to look pale and worn. "Come on in. This is Janet Mackenzie."

Janet turned and held out her hand to the two

women. She smiled with a warmth that encompassed them both, and her bright blue eyes sparkled as well-worn crow's-feet crinkled her cheeks. Her silvery white hair spoke of a greater age than her straight back and perfect figure suggested. She wore a rust-colored suit that brought out the healthy glow of her skin.

"Paula, I am very happy to meet you. We are so grateful for what you've done for Ned. Dr. Levinthal says you saved his life."

Paula took the woman's hand, disoriented by Janet's apparently intimate connection with Ned. Was she a relative? Paula tried to remember the litany of family members Ned had rattled off for her, but she couldn't recall a Janet. The woman's smile looked somewhat familiar, and she obviously felt a proprietary concern for Ned, so Paula assumed she must be an aunt that Ned had failed to mention.

"Ned, I'm going to go on back to the house. Mack will probably be here to see you this after-noon. Do you want him to bring you anything?"

"No thanks, Janet." Ned spoke softly, obviously still feeling ill.

"Should I go pick up Hector?"

Sarah broke in. "I can bring him to you, if you want, but he's welcome to stay with us until Ned is able to take care of him again."

All three women looked at Ned expectantly, but he had leaned back against the pillows and closed his eyes, apparently sleeping again. Janet smiled fondly at him and shrugged her shoulders. "Why don't you keep Hector for now until I get things organized? Mack and I are staying at Ned's house and we can come and pick up Hector later on this afternoon. We'll be here until Ned gets back on his feet, so don't worry about anything."

Paula listened to Janet's plan with confusion and a sense of loss she couldn't understand. She had been worried about how she would take care of him and manage her work at the same time. Now that dilemma had been solved, but she noticed a resentment building that this unknown person would just swoop into Ned's life and take over. She also felt somewhat embarrassed that she had called herself "the closest thing he has to family," when clearly that was not at all the case.

Sarah arranged for Janet to retrieve Hector while Paula walked quietly to Ned's side and picked up his hand. His right hand was still connected to the IV, and she noticed the slight bruising beginning around the tape holding in the needle. She squeezed the fingers of his left hand and he opened his eyes again.

"Hi." He grinned. "Every time I look up, I see you."

"I think we're going to go now and let you rest," she answered.

He gripped her hand with surprising strength, considering that he looked as if he barely had the energy to keep breathing. "I wish you would stay a little. I want to talk to you."

"Don't worry. I'll be back."

Janet interrupted them. "I think we ought to leave now. Ned, I know you love company, but rest is the best thing for you."

He rolled his eyes and sighed. "Yes, ma'am." He tried to sit up straighter and grimaced a little at the pain. "I want to get out of here as soon as possible, so I promise to be good." He squeezed Paula's hand one more time and let her go.

As the women walked down the hall toward the elevator, Janet once again thanked Paula for her role in helping Ned. "I certainly wouldn't want anything to happen to him. He has been the most wonderful son-in-law any woman could ever want."

"Son-in-law?" Paula's stomach turned over in a twist of anxiety.

Janet looked at her with compassion. "I guess you didn't realize that I'm Annie's mother."

"I—I'm sorry. No. I didn't ever hear her maiden name. I should have recognized you, though. I can see the resemblance. I thought I recognized your smile." Paula shut her mouth in a determined effort not to babble anymore and tried to smile at Janet, who seemed totally oblivious to Paula's discomfort.

Sarah jumped in and began asking Janet questions about when she had arrived from Cleveland, and if she needed anything at the house. With Sarah keeping the conversation going, the women finally arrived at the parking lot, and Janet left them to find her own car. In a haze of hurt feelings Paula wandered around looking for her car while Sarah stood watching her. Finally Sarah caught up with her friend and steered her back to where she had passed her automobile twice already.

"Open the door, Paula, and let it start warming up. Then tell me what's wrong with you."

Obeying automatically, Paula pulled out her keys, dropping Ned's house key in the process. She picked it up from the icy slush and held it in her gloved hand, staring silently at it. Tears of exhaustion, frustration, and heartache blurred her vision and began spilling down her cold cheeks. Sarah took the car keys, opened the doors, started the car, and pushed Paula into the front seat.

"Now. What's wrong?"

Paula leaned her head on the steering wheel and let herself cry until she could control herself enough to explain. "I know I am being totally irrational, Sarah. But I feel so jealous of that woman that I wanted to scratch her eyes out. I wanted to shout at her, to tell her to leave Ned alone. I know that's wrong. My gosh, the woman's daughter died, and I'm sure that Ned has been a great comfort to her. I make myself sick with feeling jealous." She heaved a sigh and shook her head. "This is the first time since I've known him that Ned has let me do anything for him, and I was looking forward to the chance to help him. Now she's here, and I'm out of the picture again. I know it doesn't make any sense, but that's how I feel. It's immature and selfish, and I'm sorry."

Sarah put her arm around Paula's shoulder and removed it immediately when Paula winced in pain. "Sorry. I forgot that you're hurt, too. You know, you and Ned are just alike. Both of you ignore your own pain and jump in trying to help others. You should probably be home sleeping off painkillers, and instead you're out here complaining that you won't get a big enough share of the burden of taking care of Ned Andersen, who promises to be the world's worst patient. Isn't that a little too much martyrdom even for you?"

"Oh, shut up, Sarah," Paula said, laughing. "Let's just go back to your house and fill up on Hector kisses before Janet takes him home."

Chapter Twelve

To Paula's surprise, she found herself unable to dislike Janet Mackenzie after all. Shortly after arriving back at Sarah's, Paula received a call from Janet asking advice about what things to take to Ned at the hospital. When Janet asked what toothbrush to take, Paula couldn't decide if Janet was simply trying to make Paula feel included, or if she was trying to determine how well Paula actually knew Ned. Paula couldn't help laughing and asked, "Just exactly how many toothbrushes does he have, Janet?"

"There are two of them in the bathroom, and I have no idea which one is his."

"Well, maybe we'd better get him a new one because one of those must be Hector's." Paula giggled.

"Oh." Janet remained silent for a minute. "I thought one might be yours."

Paula felt one brief flash of temptation to release all of her frustrations on this woman whose daughter

had held Ned's heart for so long. She wanted to
shout unkindly, "It's probably Annie's! Nothing
else of her's is gone." But in the same instant Paula
felt a surprising compassion for vibrantly alive Janet
Mackenzie, who had had to live with the pain of her
child's death and now probably feared losing her
son-in-law. Ned must be Janet's closest link to
her daughter, and she must live in dread of some
other woman taking him away. In that moment Paula
finally let go of her jealousy toward Annie. She
couldn't yet explain her relationship with Ned, but
she could at least reassure Janet.

"Nope," she said simply. "It's not mine. But if
it's not Hector's, it's probably what Ned uses to
clean the grit out from behind the faucet. Can you
believe how clean that house is?"

Both of them laughed, and Paula felt the delicate
beginning of a bond being forged with Janet. Their
mutual love for Ned could be a bridge between them
instead of a barrier of jealousy and resentment, if
they could stop being afraid that Ned only had room
in his heart for one of them.

"Janet, why don't I bring Hector back to the
house, and then I can drive you to the hospital this
afternoon. I'll be coming that way anyhow, since I'll
be staying at my own place instead of here."

When Paula pulled into the drive at Ned's house,
Hector jumped from the car to greet Janet and Mack
at the door. He knew them well and loved them, but
he returned to lay his head on Paula's feet as soon
as she sat on the sofa. The Mackenzies treated Paula
with a kind of delicate caution, waiting for her to
lead the conversation to Ned; however, Paula found
herself unable to talk about him at all. Her relationship with him had undergone so many shifts in the
past few weeks that she presumed nothing. Except

for the few brief words in the hospital, they had not even spoken for nearly three weeks.

Mack offered to drive them all to the hospital, since Paula's shoulder remained obviously painful, but then he immediately deferred to her decision saying, "Whatever you would prefer, of course."

"That would be very helpful, Mack. I'm not much use right now," she admitted ruefully.

"I think you've been very helpful to Ned, Paula," he answered as they headed for the car. "Dr. Levinthal told Janet that you stayed with Ned and helped him after the surgery. He's lucky to have you."

Feeling uncomfortable again, Paula tried to deflect the conversation saying only, "We're friends, Mack. He would have done the same for me. In fact . . ." She told them about the tornado last summer, and how Ned had helped her overcome her panic attacks. Janet nodded her head, saying simply, "That sounds like Ned."

They traded other stories of Ned's kindness, although they still skirted his ultimate kindness toward their daughter. By the time they reached Ned's room, Paula and the Mackenzies had moved past their initial awkwardness and could converse with the ease of any new acquaintances who have a common friend.

Entering the room, Janet immediately crossed over to hug Ned, and Mack shook the hand not bound to the IV. They hovered around his bed, commenting on his pallor and wondering what the surgeon thought. Ned reassured them, but his eyes continually returned to Paula, who was standing close to the door. She knew she should simply move closer and resume her role of faithful friend, but she could only think of the promise they had made never to touch each other. While he had been unconscious, she had held and kissed his hand, and when he had awakened he had touched her face, but he had been too ill for the contact to mean anything more than general human concern. Now she felt all the old pulls on her heart, and she knew she could not trust herself to give him a sisterly hug and a pat on the back.

Finally Ned broke her silence with a question about her shoulder.

"It's better now, but I won't be arm wrestling for a while."

"That's okay. I won't be able to manage your fights for a while, either. I wouldn't want you to start looking for a new manager with promises of Madison Square Garden and Las Vegas."

Mack laughed at that. "You can't mean to tell me that this tiny little squirt of a girl likes to fight?"

"She's an amazon in disguise, Mack," Ned answered. "Especially when she's fighting for a worthy cause."

Janet noticed that in spite of the bantering, Paula had remained far from the others and showed no sign of moving closer. The fluorescent glare drained Paula's face of its fragile color, leaving her nearly as pale as Ned and looking lost and alone. Glancing back at Ned, Janet saw a yearning sadness and wished she could ease his pain. She didn't understand the apparent strain between these two, but she thought some time alone might help them.

"Mack, come down with me to the cafeteria and we'll get some coffee. I haven't had a cup all day, and I could use one."

"But we just got here, Janet," he complained.

"Mack . . ." she warned.

"I'll get you a cup, Janet," Paula interjected, and

she practically ran out of the room and down the hall.

Janet turned to Mack in exasperation. "Mack Mackenzie, you have the brain of a rock sometimes."

"What?"

"Oh never mind. I'm sorry, Ned. We'll leave for a while when she gets back. I know you'd like to have some time alone." She affectionately shoved the back of Mack's head.

"Oh, I get it." Mack wiggled his eyebrows up and down. "Why didn't you just say so?"

Ned shook his head at them. "You two are incorrigible. But don't worry about it. I'm not so sure that Paula and I need time alone, after all. There's probably not all that much left for us to say."

"Problems?" Mack asked.

"Nothing but," replied Ned. "It sometimes seems we were doomed before we ever got started. But it's my fault; I just don't know what to do about it."

"I like her, Ned," Janet said. "She could so easily resent our being here, but she has been kind and gracious. I feel so sure that she loves you."

Startled by Janet's easy acceptance of a relationship that caused him so much conflict, Ned blew out a heavy sigh. "Well, like I said, it's my fault, and I'll have to fix it."

They chatted easily about other family members until Paula returned with Janet's coffee. When Janet and Mack started to leave, Paula retained them by launching into a description of the ethanol plant and Ned's contributions. "I haven't had time to tell you Parker's good news, Ned. He got a grant from USDOE and the Ontario Corn Producers Association to work on those ethanol-driven wastewater pumps. And he's giving you all the credit for discovering that new dry grind method that solves the sulphur dioxide problem. It's wonderful news.''

''What's this, Ned?'' asked Mack.

By the time Ned explained everything to Janet and Mack, the nurse had stuck her head in the room and warned that visiting hours would be ending in a few minutes. Janet stood up to leave first, but Paula had already reached the door. ''Go ahead and say your good-byes, Janet; I'll wait outside. Bye, Ned. I'll see you later. I'm going back to school tomorrow, but you can leave a message if you need anything.'' She waved a casual salute and skipped out the door again, refusing even to look directly at Ned. She retreated halfway down the hall before she let herself stop long enough to realize she was trembling, and she had nearly reached the elevators before she asked herself why she was once again running away.

''I thought I could do this,'' she muttered to herself. ''I thought I could pretend just to be his friend. It made him happy; it makes Janet happy, and it seemed better than not seeing him at all. But I can't do it any more. I can't do it. I can't keep skirting around the edges of his life and running away every time my feelings become to strong.''

She flopped into a chair near the elevator doors, grunting a little at the continuing stiffness in her shoulder. Her temper flared again, and she probably would have hurt herself by hitting something in frustration, but Janet and Mack appeared, and she held herself in check.

They made the drive back to the house in silence and Paula declined their invitation to come in for some food. ''I have to be up early for school tomorrow,'' she explained. ''I'm starting a pretty busy time of the year with semester finals, so chances are I won't see you again before you leave. If you need any help, though, be sure to call me. The Bradys will also help, and I'm sure Grace or the other employees at the county office would be glad to lend a hand.''

She had already climbed into her car and started the engine when Janet knocked on the window. ''Paula,'' she started and then hesitated. ''I just wanted to let you know again how glad we are that you were here for Ned. I know that you mean a lot to him. He's been a long time getting over Annie's death, but I think you've helped him to finally move on. We're happy about that. We want him to be happy.''

Paula drove home with those words echoing in her mind. ''We want him to be happy.'' Everyone wanted Ned to be happy, including herself, but she no longer believed that she could be a part of his happiness. If he was ever going to recover from the pain of Annie's death, it apparently would not be because of Paula. It was time for her to move on, and now that he had made it safely through the surgery, she intended to do just that.

She returned to her classroom the next day, laughing at her attempts to write on the board with her left hand, and threatening anyone who made fun of her clumsiness. By Friday she had removed the sling and begun to work on strengthening exercises, but she didn't have much time to worry about regaining full use of her arm and shoulder. That afternoon as her last class finished their final exam, Mr. Reinhardt entered her classroom with a pink message slip from the office.

''I thought you ought to see this right away, Paula, and I was afraid you might not stop by the office before you left,'' he said.

''Thanks,'' she said as she glanced curiously at

the note. It was from Janet, and it requested that she come by Ned's house as soon as she finished work. Paula looked at her principal in confusion and worry. "Did you talk to her? Did she say anything else?"

"Sorry, Paula, the student who answers the phone at lunchtime took the message. I hope everything is all right."

"Maybe I should go right away." She looked around the room at the stacks of paperwork that had begun accumulating since her two days' absence, and the exam papers that needed to be graded.

"Paula, go ahead. I know you will get things done eventually, and right now it sounds like you're needed elsewhere."

Paula looked at Mr. Reinhardt with relief. Occasionally he slipped out of his slave-driver role long enough to be a very nice human being, reminding Paula of why she continued to want to work here. "If you could just help me pick up this stack of papers to put in my briefcase, I can at least take them with me to look at over the weekend."

Soon she was headed out of town along the river road, marveling at the amount of daylight still left and distracting herself from worries about Ned by searching for signs of life in the snow and ice. When she parked in front of the house, Hector and Janet both ran out to meet her.

"Oh, Paula, I'm so glad to see you. I was so worried I didn't know what I would do if you didn't make it." Janet was practically pulling Paula into the house as she spoke. Inside the door, two large suitcases stood against the wall with Janet's coat draped over the top of them. She had apparently been laying a fire in the fireplace, and she returned to complete her task as she continued to explain.

"Ned is being discharged today! Can you believe

that? Anyway, Mack and I can't stay after all. Our
son's wife is having a baby, and he called last night
to tell us she thinks it's going to come early. So of
course, Mack and I have to go back home to be with
them. We thought we would have enough time to
help Ned here and then get back in time, but everything's changed, and I'm so grateful that you're here
because otherwise I would feel terrible leaving Ned
alone when he's still so sick.'' She talked without
taking a breath, as if she had to hurry and say everything at once before Paula interrupted her with any
questions.

Finally she stopped speaking, but she kept her
back to Paula as she put the finishing touches
on the stacked wood. Paula felt completely out-
maneuvered, and she didn't even understand exactly
what Janet had gained.

''Janet . . .''

''There now. You can have a nice fire going to
keep you warm. There are plenty of groceries in the
kitchen, if you don't mind putting things in the oven
to warm them up. I know your shoulder still hurts,
but don't you think you'll be able to manage? After
all, you've been taking care of yourself for a few
days now. Ned can't be that much trouble.''

''Janet . . .'' Paula tried again to ask what was going on, but just then another car sounded in the
drive.

''Oh, wonderful! They're here. Mack and I will
have time to get back home before it's late.''

''Janet!''

But the front door was opening and Mack was
walking a weak and unhappy Ned through the front
door. Paula had her one good arm full grabbing
Hector and preventing him from jumping up on his
master. Helping Ned to the sofa, Mack sent Janet

running for pillows and a blanket, and ordered Paula to hold Hector until the patient was settled. Paula knelt beside the animal, who quieted immediately, and watched Ned's face as the Mackenzies fussed and fluttered around him. Finally he had been coddled to their satisfaction, and as they backed away from him in contentment Paula released Hector's collar.

To her amazement Hector remained beside her rather than leaping to Ned as she had expected. Only when she released him with a "Go on, Hector," did he walk carefully to the sofa to stick his nose in Ned's face. Their reunion touched her heart, and she felt her resolve weaken once again with the strength of her feelings for Ned.

"Well, we're off then," Mack called from the door. "Give us a call and let us know how you're doing."

Paula practically raced to the door, but they were quicker than she, and Mack had the suitcases on the front porch before Paula could stop him. "But you can't leave him here like this!" she exclaimed. "He's still too weak to take care of himself, Janet."

"Of course he is, dear. That's why I called you. You'll know just what to do for him. Now you make him mind you and don't let him go back to work too soon. The instructions for his postoperative care are with those discharge papers on the table." Janet gave her a hug. "I'm so glad we met, Paula," she whispered. "Even if the circumstances have been difficult. Next time we'll just have some fun together."

"Good-bye, Ned. We love you!" they called out, and then they were gone.

Paula stood looking dazedly after them as if she expected Mack to turn the car around and come back in laughing at the joke they had all had on Paula. But they didn't return, and eventually the cold air coming through the open door jarred her from her reverie so that she closed the door and returned to the living room. Ned still held Hector's head on his chest, but he twisted around to watch Paula as she entered the room and picked up the papers.

"Paula, I'm sorry about this. I had no idea that they were leaving today or I would have made some arrangements myself. I still can."

She flopped into the armchair across the room from him and absently stroked Hector's head when he came and placed it in her lap. "Don't be silly, Ned. I certainly don't mind helping you out if you don't mind having me around."

Ned started to answer, then frowned and shut his eyes as if he were controlling himself. With a sigh he replied, "You know that I don't mind having you around. Having you around is one of the best parts of my life."

She concentrated on scratching behind Hector's ears, forcing herself not to look at Ned. When he said something like that, it made her heart leap with hope, and she knew she couldn't afford to continue to hope that this relationship would finally be allowed to grow. Abruptly she rose from the chair and stalked off toward the kitchen. "Those papers said something about a liquid diet for several days. Have you been able to eat anything yet?"

"I've been able to eat, I just don't have much appetite." Ned watched her as she moved nervously through the house. Clearly she felt uncomfortable being here, and he wondered if the strain on them during the past few months had destroyed the love she had had before. Her absence for the past several weeks had left a tremendous void in his life, and he had truly thought he would never see her again. In spite of the conflicts in his heart, he knew that he cherished her as the most important person in his life. Somehow Janet's easy acceptance of Paula encouraged Ned to believe he could overcome his guilt feelings, but for the first time he questioned if she still felt for him the same commitment he felt for her.

"How about some soup?" she called from the kitchen. "That shouldn't be too hard on you."

"Anything is all right, Paula," he assured her, but she slapped a can opener down on the counter and moved to stand in the doorway to the living room.

"Ned Andersen, you're going to have to learn how to be a good patient."

"What do you mean?" he asked in a hurt voice. "I'm trying not to be too much trouble!"

"That's not what a good patient does. A good patient lets the nurse provide care. He says what he wants and then when she gets it for him, he is appropriately grateful. A good patient does *not* act as if he doesn't need anything. That only makes the nurse feel unappreciated." She stood with her hands clenched on her hips and scowled at him. "Got it?"

"Okay. Okay. I've got it." He laughed. "Let's see. Soup would be absolutely perfect. If you wouldn't mind making some hot tea, I think I would like that as well. Is that better?"

"Much." She hesitated a minute before continuing. "Do you think that their daughter-in-law is really going into labor, or did they just know something I don't know about how bad a patient you could be?"

"They know me pretty well. I'd say you've been set up."

"I should have known." She sighed, rolling her eyes.

The bantering returned them to their normal joking interaction, and while the soup warmed, Ned relaxed enough to nap. Paula lit the fire Janet had laid, and the room took on a warm, comforting glow as night closed in around them. Hector made do without his run, but Paula was able to throw some left-handed tosses of the tennis ball to help him use up some of his excess energy. After they had eaten Paula graded papers, and Ned pretended to read until he again fell asleep. She worried about how tired he remained, but she let him sleep, assuming he must need the rest. The quiet house, disturbed only by the slight crackling of the fire and the gentle snoring of both Ned and Hector, filled her with a sense of peace and security, an illusion of the permanence she had so often wanted. She let the last of her papers float to the floor and her eyes closed in slumber.

Her neck and shoulder both hurt ferociously when she awoke the next morning, but she soon worked the kinks out by busying herself in the kitchen fixing breakfast. When Ned stirred a short time later, she helped him climb the stairs to clean up.

"Are you sure you feel strong enough for this?" she asked.

"If I don't get a shower today, I'm going to be too strong even for myself! I always thought that a beautiful nurse was supposed to give you a sponge bath in the hospital."

"Boy are you living in the wrong half of the twentieth century!" She shoved him gently into the bathroom. "And don't expect this nurse to give you a bath, either. You can just do that yourself."

While Ned showered, Paula refilled the bird feeders she and Ned had placed around the yard during the late fall. Mack and Janet had probably been too busy even to notice them, but Paula knew that the creatures would be desperate for food in this ice and snow. Thinking of the effort to pour in the seed as a kind of exercise for her shoulder, Paula ignored the pain until she had completed the job. By the time she returned to the house, she felt exhausted with her efforts.

She finished steeping a pot of breakfast tea and stood at the window, drinking a cup of the hot, sweet liquid and watching the sparrows and chickadees crowding the surfaces of the feeders. Other winter inhabitants began to swarm by, adding the blues and reds of jays, juncos, and cardinals. The finches were so muted in their winter colors that they looked like siblings of the sparrows. Paula wondered if the feeders would be emptied by the raccoons and opossums before the birds managed to have their fill, and she thought about releasing Hector to play guard duty.

"That smells good," Ned said behind her. "I'm almost hungry, and if I don't run out of energy, I'll try to be a good patient and eat what you've fixed."

She knew he stood very close, and she held herself still, unwilling to face him. "The birds seem to be happy with what I gave them. Maybe you should try your oats dry like they do if the oatmeal isn't any good."

"I will be happy with anything you give me." She heard the meaning behind the words but forced herself to ignore them and remain silent.

Finally she felt him back off, and she turned around. "Go be comfortable by the fire and I'll bring you a tray."

They had reestablished the rules for now. She certainly wouldn't abandon Ned while he needed her, but she would not allow this reversal of their former roles to persuade her that their relationship had actually changed. Annie's picture continued to dominate the living room, and Annie's ring had been returned to its place on Ned's finger.

Later in the afternoon, Ned seemed to lose some of the ground he had gained, and Paula insisted he get in bed. When she checked his temperature she found he was running a fever again. A call to the after-care nurse resulted in Dr. Levinthal prescribing a second course of antibiotics to prevent the feared peritonitis. Paula wondered if she should return Ned to the hospital, but Dr. Levinthal had great faith in her ability to care for his patient.

"Keep him still for a couple more days, but elevate and move his legs. Once he starts on the antibiotics, he should be better in a day, but the course of treatment runs for ninety-six hours. If he complains of nausea or abdominal swelling, call me immediately. Think you can handle it?"

Paula assured him she could manage and left soon after to pick up the medicine and some clothes for herself. If she was to remain with Ned for at least four days, she intended to have clean clothes to wear. The temperature had dropped again, and heavy snow clouds began releasing a steady, silent flow of tiny flakes. By the time Paula headed back out of town, the precipitation had become so heavy that she had difficulty seeing, and only her familiarity with the route allowed her to avoid running off the narrow road.

Ned appeared to be no worse, but he remained listless and feverish as she prepared some beef broth and toast to accompany his medication. Throughout the night, Paula tiptoed into his room to touch his forehead and listen to his breathing, and finally she simply curled up beside Hector on the rug. With the first light of dawn she crept back downstairs to prepare a tray for him.

Dr. Levinthal's prediction proved correct, and Ned began to improve rapidly again. Paula bullied him into remaining in bed, and she helped him exercise his legs to prevent blood clots. Ned laughed at her whenever she became too bossy. "Now I understand how your students must feel. I always wondered how such a short little thing could control those gigantic high school boys, but now I wonder why they don't all leave in fear and trembling."

"They know they're lucky to have me as their teacher!" she insisted.

"I agree. They are lucky. So am I. You've taught me how to be a good patient."

"Well at least you're making progress in that area."

The snow had continued to fall steadily all night and through the day, and when Paula took Hector out for his run, she found herself knee-deep in cold, wet fluff. Hector chased her snowballs and bit them to pieces before he could return them to her, simultaneously loving the cold on his tongue and hating the lack of substance in his prize. When they finally succumbed to the cold and returned to the house, he shook ice and melting snow in a freezing arc around the kitchen. Paula dried him off with a towel before sending him up to Ned. She cleaned the mess in the kitchen and then heated up a casserole Janet had put in the freezer.

Even as she thought of Janet, the telephone rang with a call from Ned's in-laws. Paula heard Ned answer the phone upstairs and went back to her chores. When she ascended to Ned's room some time later, he was just hanging up.

"They both said to apologize to you," he remarked as she entered with a tray.

"What for?" she asked. "Sticking me with you, or forcing me to eat Janet's incredibly good food?"

"Janet didn't give you a choice about staying here, did she?"

Paula took her own plate off the tray and sat with it across the room. "She didn't need to, and she knew it, Ned. Janet is a very astute woman, I think, and she was trying to help. But she doesn't quite understand our situation, does she?"

Ned ate in silence for a few minutes and then set his fork down as if he hadn't the energy to hold it any longer. "How could she understand our situation when I don't even understand it myself?" He hung his head as if in shame but then forced himself to look at her. "I know something needs to change, Paula. I just don't know how to do it."

Paula would not let herself be drawn into this discussion while Ned still needed her. He obviously couldn't fend for himself yet, and she would not deal with her own stress until he could.

"We're friends, Ned. I thought we established that already." As Ned's friend, she remained with him for several days, fixing meals, running Hector, feeding the birds, and even cleaning some. As Ned's friend, when the short break between semesters had ended and the snow had cleared enough for school to reopen, she returned to her own apartment with a change in the rules.

"You were right about something needing to change, Ned. I need time alone for a while," she said as they stood on the front porch of his house. "I know that I was the one who asked for this arrangement between us, but right now it isn't working. It's just too hard."

"I'm sorry, Paula. I know it's put a lot on you to take care of me these past few days." He looked chagrined at the thought that he had demanded too much of her.

Frustration finally won out, and Paula exploded with the thoughts she had been harboring since the night of his telephone call. "It's not that you put a lot on me, Ned! You don't put enough on me. Finally, after all these months, you allow me to give you something in return for all that you have given me, and I have relished every minute of it. *That* is the problem. I love being able to help you. I love being able to be with you like this. I love being your helpmate and partner. I love it so much that I can't stand the fact that it isn't real. Now that you're back on your feet, we will go back to the same old routine of you being totally self-sufficient and emotionally isolated. I thought that I could be your friend. I thought that I would overcome all the other things that I wanted from you because your friendship is worth it. I want to be able to do that, Ned. I want to be that self-sacrificing, noble woman, but I'm not. I love you, and it hurts too much to keep telling myself that my love for you is not allowed."

"Paula, you know I love you, too. I just—"

She interrupted him. "It's not enough, Ned. Not now. I need to get away from this for now." She walked to the car and drove away without looking at him again.

Rather than allow herself to mope about at home, Paula threw herself into her work. She developed a wildlife management protocol for the plant site that included teaching goals for her environmental science class and for her general biology students. No longer did she rush through her papers in order to have free time at night. Instead she found herself dragging out her day as long as possible in order to limit the amount of time she might spend thinking about Ned. She stayed at the school building so late on several evenings that Mr. Reinhardt called her in to his office and suggested that she leave earlier.

"After all, Paula, we can't have the local citizens thinking that you are out here conducting some unauthorized experiment on school property."

Paula wanted to become angry with him and argue that she wouldn't need to work late if she had adequate preparation time during the day, but she knew that the late hours were actually her own choice. She tried slowing down her work then, but only succeeded in taking more papers home to grade. The dark, cold misery of February passed slowly and Paula still refused to contact Ned.

Ned recuperated little by little, but he did so almost against his will. By the beginning of March he had returned full time to work, but he found himself unable to last the long hours he had previously spent as a way of avoiding his personal pain. Instead of scrubbing the house and chopping firewood, he spent hours sitting quietly in front of the fireplace, staring into the flames and stroking Hector's soft head. He dreamt of Paula. He dreamt of Annie. Sometimes he dreamt of someone and awoke not knowing which woman had filled his sleep, only knowing that he awoke with a disquiet that would not leave him even when he had been awake for hours.

Winter finally gave way to spring and he received one call from Paula. "I'm going to visit my mother for the week of spring vacation," she explained. "I thought maybe we could get together when I return."

"Are you all right?" he asked with concern. Her

voice sounded low, discouraged and he wondered if her mother's condition had worsened.

"I'm fine. Mama's not any better, but she seems to have reached a temporary plateau. I miss her a lot."

"I understand."

"I know you do. I guess that's why I called. Somehow I don't seem to be able to stop letting you help me."

He smiled when he heard the irritation in her voice. She hated seeming weak, and she would fight it, but in the end she accepted help with much better grace than he.

"I'll see you when you get back," he offered.

"Thanks."

She headed into the humid warmth of the Georgia spring, hoping that she would once more find the strengthening tonic of her mother's love and example.

Chapter Thirteen

Ned attempted to stretch his legs in the cramped space between the seats of the 747. The flight to Tucson from Cleveland wore on interminably, leaving him tired and irritable. The seats felt like boulders covered with burlap, the colorless space beyond the windows gave the impression of some sensory deprivation chamber, and the steady drone of the engine had taken on the torturous quality of a dentist's drill. Ned hadn't wanted to come on this trip anyway, and he had fobbed it off on Karen Rendquist until she had called the night before with a fever of 102 degrees.

He worried about Paula returning to Preston to find him gone. He had left a message on her answering machine, but he never trusted the things to work. He also worried about Hector, although Hector probably had Sarah Brady serving him filet mignon right now. Mostly he worried about how he

would survive the next five days of listening to research papers on wastewater treatment innovations
without a distraction from the depression that had
hit him so hard these past two months.

The captain's voice crackled an announcement
about landing preparation, and Ned felt the shifting
thrust as the flaps descended. The cold grayness disappeared to be replaced by a starkly blue sky and
the rust-red and purple of the desert mountains. Ned
leaned closer to the window and suddenly imagined
Paula laughing at his irritable mood. How fitting, she
would say, that he would come to the desert to learn
about caring for water.

An hour later he drove his rented car up the wind-
ing drive to the entrance of the El Conquistador Resort where the conference was being held. *Well* he
thought, *the producers of equipment certainly do intend to treat us poor consumers nicely on this trip.*
The red-roofed cottages nestled along the hillside
gave the illusion of a small Mexican village, but the
main hotel boasted every appointment of luxury.
With a smile at the fate that forced him into a five-
day stay in such beauty, Ned parked the car, registered, and moved into his room.

The conference proceeded typically and Ned actually became enthusiastic about the new membrane
filters being used in Japan. Long interested in the
products of Mizu Technologies, Ned always sought
out their sales booth to peruse the latest designs. He
had originally thought the membranes were only
suitable for the experiment he had suggested to
Parker Mills, but now he thought they might be
adaptable for the tiny unincorporated towns in his
county that had no better sewerage treatment than a
widened spot in the river allowing waste products to
sift to the bottom.

Hovering around the membrane demonstration, Ned found himself face to face with Kazuo Yamamoto, the Mizu sales rep and Ned's friend since college days.

"Ah, It's Ned Ander-san." Kazuo smiled easily.

Ned remembered how Yamamoto loved to make English-Japanese puns, and groaned, "No, Kazuo, please. No puns."

The two men shook hands and spent several minutes catching up on recent events in their various careers. Although they had known each other for years, neither had ever intruded on the other's personal life. Yamamoto had known Annie, since she also had been part of the environmental science department, but he had never socialized with either Ned or Annie. Now he saw with concern that his friend looked worn with fatigue and stress. Yamamoto wanted to express his concern, but not so overtly that Ned would be offended.

"Ander-san, why don't you come to my cottage this afternoon after the poster session. My wife, Takie, is there and she will serve us tea. Can I introduce can I?"

"What? I don't understand"

"Sorry, Ned. Another pun. *Kanai* is Japanese for 'my wife.' I would like for you to meet her."

Ned's eyes widened with surprise, but he gratefully accepted. Every minute he kept busy meant another minute safe from feelings he wanted to avoid. Ned had never attended an authentic Japanese tea ceremony.

Walking up the gently sloped hill to Yamamoto's quarters, Ned wondered when he had become so completely exhausted. He felt as if he carried tremendous weights on his shoulders and arms, but he couldn't account for the weariness. Surely it was simply the change in air pressure from Ohio, or perhaps unexpected jet lag.

He entered the small guest cottage, stepping out of the warm afternoon sun into the cool, dark interior. Like all of the cottages, the red tile roof and white stucco walls complemented the southwestern decor of the rooms; however, somehow Yamamoto's possession of the cottage had resulted in a slightly Eastern impression. Three small, woven wool rugs leaned against a closet door, and a reed mat had been spread out in their place. A low glass coffee table, which apparently belonged in front of the sofa, had been crowded into the hallway leading to the bedrooms.

Yamamoto greeted his friend, gesturing to him to sit on the floor beside the mat, and a few minutes later Takie brought in a tray containing articles for the preparation of the tea. Ned watched with fascination as she lowered herself onto her knees without any suggestion that she might lose her balance.

"Do you understand the tradition of the tea ceremony, Ned?" Yamamoto asked.

"Not at all. I hope you won't let me commit a social blunder, Kazuo."

"No. That is not important, anyway, Ned. As a guest, you must simply allow the moment for refreshment and contemplation. Watch Takie; she is an artist."

As Ned watched Takie's gently swirling movements, brushing the green tea in the tiny bowl, he found himself absorbed with her flowing movements. Her perfect quiet, the serenity of her face and body, the soft scraping of the brush transported him to a place of utter tranquility.

With a jerk, he opened his eyes, seeing two small teacups place before himself and Yamamoto. Takie had disappeared into some other region of the cottage, and Ned felt the flush of embarrassment creeping up his neck. He started to apologize until he saw the faint beginnings of a smile on his friend's face.

"Always one learns from the proper appreciation of art. I knew you would appreciate Takie's art, Ned. Later you will discover what you have learned." He spoke matter of factly, as if having a guest fall asleep during tea occurred every day. "So drink your tea and then we will walk and talk about the new membranes."

When Ned returned to his own room later, he forced himself to replay his memory of the afternoon. Yamamoto might be a thoroughly successful businessman, who knew American culture well enough to glide easily in any social situation, but he also retained a deep personal connection to his Japanese culture. Ned understood that the tea ceremony had been a gift from an old friend who could see that Ned needed something. But what did he need? Sleep?

That didn't seem to be the right answer. Ned didn't need sleep, he needed . . . peace. That was what he had felt for those few moments while he watched Takie prepare the tea. He needed peace, and he had not experienced it for many years now.

Opening his curtains, he watched the last faint smudges of orange and purple light playing out over the tops of the mountains surrounding the vast desert valley. He remembered a trip he had taken here the summer before he graduated from college. He had planned to ask Annie to marry him when he returned to campus, but they both had wanted to spend that last summer of youth traveling independently. Annie's parents had sent her to Europe, and Ned had borrowed his brother's motorcycle to travel west. When he reached the Arizona desert he spent the rest of his time climbing among the arroyos and renting a horse to follow the trail guides into the mountains. He never even made it to California.

With the conviction of absolute certainty, Ned knew he needed to climb into those mountains again. Whatever might bring him lasting peace he would find out in that desert. Flipping through the conference schedule, Ned calculated just how many sessions he could miss without committing an ethical breech. Fortunately, the conference planners assumed that the attendees would all want to enjoy the location, and the last day's activities ended at noon. With a quick check of the presentation titles, Ned discovered that he could take an entire day without missing anything he hadn't already read. He smiled to himself in anticipation of an entire day alone in those hills.

Passing beyond the resort's stables early the next morning, Ned found the roughly marked hiking trail leading into the mountains. He knew enough about the toxic effects of desert plants to wear protective clothing, but otherwise he felt completely out of his element. The desert could have been another planet, so different was it from the lush green fields of Ohio. He rejoiced in this difference, this starkness that shook him from his habitual thoughts and actions.

Climbing the eroding stone at the base of the mountain, Ned remembered how distorting size and distance were in this vastness. From his window in the hotel, the base of the hills looked like a gentle slope that could easily be walked, but the reality was a slippery and exhausting trek up a considerable distance. He climbed for nearly an hour through the cacti and scrub brush before finally resting on the rocky slope. He felt somewhat lightheaded and realized he had gone too long without water.

He reached for one of the three bottles he had packed in his rucksack, checked the ground for poisonous critters, and sat viewing the open wilderness. The desert clarified things. Every nonessential aspect of life had been stripped away in the struggle for survival. The dry air showed edges unmodified by the blurring of vapor. Clarified, purged, purified. The desert allowed no illusions. If you walked here ignoring painful realities, you would most likely die.

Ned allowed the reality of the desert to enter his mind. He needed to clarify himself, and he knew that meant purging himself of his own illusions. He felt disgusted with himself for his inability even to understand what was wrong, but he knew he had somehow built up a system of defenses that now threatened to strangle him.

He swallowed the warming water and placed the bottle beside him, thinking again of the beauty of the water conference being held in the desert where the substance was so precious. In a rainy state like Ohio, people took clean water for granted too easily, but since Ned had first come to the desert, he had known how valuable a resource it was. Knowing that he cleaned the community's water gave him a transcendental gratification that he never spoke of because he feared it would sound so ridiculous. But he knew no greater satisfaction than realizing that he helped clear out the detritus of civilization to repurify the life-giving substance.

Now Ned felt as if his own life needed that kind of purification. He seemed to move through an ever-thickening world of sludge, and he longed for the peace of clarity. He had fought this moment for so long, but now he knew he had to face the waste products of his own life and remove them once and for all.

"Annie." He breathed the word as if hoping she could somehow save him from this. She couldn't. She was part of it.

When had it started? An image rose automatically. *Annie reaching for his hand, grinning, nervous, framed in pastel colors.* He remembered that day. *After months of trying to conceive a baby, they were so certain she was finally pregnant. Now they waited in the examination room for her gynecologist to return with confirmation. She glowed with excitement, and Ned was so certain that only pregnancy could make her look that beautiful when she had been feeling so ill.*

Another image replaced the first. *He noticed every detail of the Impressionist print on the wall of the physician's office. What was he thinking? Ah yes, how Impressionists should be damned to the inner circles of hell. How grotesque pastel wallpaper was. How grateful he was that the older hospital did not bother to decorate the chemotherapy department, so he would only have to confront the ugly starkness of chrome, black, and white. And most shameful of all, how much he hated all those smiling, pregnant women in the waiting room.*

Ned wrenched himself from the memory, not willing to re-experience the pain. But the desert held him captive. He would find no release here, no distracting business, no compulsive work to fend off the past. He forced himself back again.

The anger. How he had wanted to unleash that anger. *He needed to break something. He wanted to kill something. He wanted something else to die . . . not Annie. But something happened to that anger. He saw her face again. This time frightened. So fear-*

*ful. She didn't fear her death; she feared his anger.
She feared what his anger would do to him, to them.
And so he had hidden it.* He had buried it so deeply
he had actually thought it was gone. Only once had
he felt it strike again with its poisonous fang. The
day he had seen Paula holding Kevin. She had suddenly become such an omnipotent threat that the anger had broken from its prison and he had nearly
struck her.

Even now Ned couldn't understand the anger.
What could Paula have threatened in him? She had
never been anything but loving and kind, but she had
frightened him to the point that the anger had nearly
escaped. The desert held no answers; only the past
knew those.

Paula's words from her mother's bedside had re-
vived those last terrible weeks when Annie, betrayed
by that beautiful body, had wasted away to nothing
but pain. Finally not even the pain existed, only
massive doses of morphine and thorazine, as the hos-
pice nurse increased the doses in an effort to relieve
Annie's suffering. Ned forced himself to relive that
last vigil when he had sat for hours listening to every
breath, not knowing how to keep himself from wishing it would all be over. He took himself back
through the desperate shame he had felt when he
realized he had stayed with her all those nights, only
to fall asleep just before the end.

What had happened then? He couldn't remember.
Ned wondered at the irony of a memory that retained
every detail of Annie's suffering but failed him when
he tried to retrieve the time when she had finally
been released. He knew Annie's parents had come
to be with him and that he had somehow helped
them through their own loss, but he couldn't remember any of the conversations they had had.

The bright morning sun began penetrating the dark memories holding Ned and he searched through the backpack for sunscreen. Applying it liberally to his exposed skin, he then shouldered the pack and continued up the nearly invisible trail. Were it not for the occasional painted marker, he would have been off the route dozens of times. He sniffed the combination of sunscreen and sand, the odor transporting him back to the week his in-laws had dragged him to their cottage on Lake Erie.

Picking up his pace, Ned ignored the blazing heat and shoved himself through the broken rocks. He stumbled, pressed on, moving his legs more swiftly, but unable to make much progress across the slippery shale. Sunlight glinted on the reflective rock, burning his eyes with the glare. He stumbled again, fell, and cut his hand on the sharp rock. A small drop of blood welled up, captivating his attention and insisting that he face the vision that had been chasing him.

Throwing himself down in despair, Ned lay on the hillside with his arm slung over his face. He didn't even know why he resisted thinking about that week; he only knew that every time he had started to remember it, he had banished the memory to the farthest corner of his mind. He steadied his breathing, eventually allowing his pulse to return to normal, willing himself to be calm. The drop of blood on his palm had already coagulated and he wiped it with his handkerchief, causing the cut to bleed again.

Annie's mother, Janet, cut herself while peeling potatoes for dinner. Ned watched her from across the kitchen, wondering how she could care enough to try to eat. He brought her a towel to wipe off the blood, holding it out to her without expression.

"Why do you bother, Janet?" he finally asked. *"I certainly can't eat, and I don't think you can either."*

"I will make myself eat, Ned, until the time comes that I can enjoy it again."

He stared at her in disbelief. "Enjoy? Without Annie there won't ever be joy."

Then she took his face in her hands and told him.

Ned sat up, not seeing the rocks or the cactus, but feeling Janet's hands on his face. What had she said to him? *"As long as you hold her in your heart, she won't ever truly be dead."*

Why did that phrase cut him so? It was the kind of thing people said to each other when they couldn't think of anything else to say. It was a platitude of the worst kind in the face of a loved one's death. What did it matter what Janet had said?

It mattered because he believed it.

Ned's heart pounded ferociously. His mouth felt as dry as the desert ground. The weights he had noticed on his shoulders and arms tripled in mass, and he could barely breathe. He believed Janet's words. *"As long as you hold her in your heart, she won't ever truly be dead."* In all those long months of Annie's illness, no one had given him a single course of action that would stave off her death. Nothing more could be done. The helplessness had devastated him in the most profound way possible. Nothing he did mattered, because nothing he did could stop Annie from dying. But as long as he held her in his heart, he could keep her spirit alive inside himself. That he could do, and that he had done.

The mountains resumed their clarity. Ned once more became aware of the sharp edges on which he sat, and the scorching heat burning his face. Gulping more of his water, he wondered briefly if perhaps he should simply allow himself to die up here. It wouldn't be all that difficult. Just throw away the rest of his water and keep walking up the mountain. He would become dehydrated and disoriented fairly quickly, he knew. He might even die from a rattlesnake bite or a poisoned jab from one of the plants. But he didn't really want to die. He knew that. He laughed sardonically even as he removed the lid from the sunscreen. He didn't want to die or even get a sunburn. He just wanted to feel better.

Down the path he saw movement. At first he thought it was a deer or a dog. Then suddenly a huge jackrabbit, its ears at least as high as Ned's waist, bounded into full view and then vanished into the brush. A shadow passed overhead, revealing the broad wings of an auburn Harris hawk gliding out to meet his brothers. A slight shimmer to the right, and a Western fence lizard broke from his frozen stance to slither away across the rocks, his bluish gray scales differentiating him from his brown Ohio cousin. Alerted by another flutter, Ned recognized the compact brown featherball of the house wren perched on the tip of a bitterbrush plant. Even in the desert those hardy, tiny birds managed to find homes. Even in this desolation, life fought and won. Ned wanted to live, too.

Why couldn't he move on? "You can't let her out of your heart." The words that came to his mind might have been spoken aloud, so clearly did he hear them. Realization flooded him. If he allowed himself to love Paula, he would let Annie out of his heart. If he no longer held her in his heart, she would truly be dead. Not only would she be dead, but it would be his fault.

The only thing he had had power over was the ability to keep her in his heart. He kept her alive with his love. If he gave that love to someone else, he might as well admit to killing her.

"Annie," he moaned. No wonder he had felt angry with Paula. She threatened his love for Annie. She threatened the only thing that kept Annie alive. "Paula." He whispered her name with equal pain. She had said she wouldn't be Annie's enemy. She had conspired with him to keep up this ludicrous charade that he had any control over Annie's death.

What was that word he had always liked so much? Hubris. Pride so profound that it didn't even recognize itself. Ned thought of another word: humility. The realistic recognition of one's limitations. For nearly six years he had rejected humility and lived a kind of unremitting hubris, never admitting the limits of his ability to control matters of life and death. He took a deep breath of the clean desert air. It was time to accept Annie's death. It was time to accept life with a little humility. He pulled the dull gold band off his finger.

Chapter Fourteen

"April is Tornado Safety Month." The poster hanging above the student lockers outside Paula's classroom proudly displayed a terrorized family huddled in the basement of their home, while a tornado proceeded to devastate the surrounding farmland.

"What a cheerful thought." She grimaced as she closed the door behind her. "Only four or five more months until the season is over." She lugged her bulging briefcase toward the staircase closest to the faculty parking lot.

"Ms. Rosewood!"

Paula halted long enough for two of her senior students to overtake her. "Ms. Rosewood, are you going out to the preserve this afternoon?" The boy and girl looked as if they desperately needed her to say yes, and Paula smiled at their urgency. Both were hoping for some extra credit as they headed into the fourth quarter of the year.

173

"I hadn't planned to, John, but I suppose I could. I can't take you without written permission from your parents, though."

"We don't need a ride, Ms. Rosewood," answered the girl, Connie. "We just need you to show us the work you do so we can help out for an extra-credit project."

Paula debated whether or not to agree to the trip. She had received a message from Parker saying Ned had returned from Arizona with some hopeful tips to increase production, and Parker wanted to meet with them that evening. Paula wanted to put some closure on this frustrating need she had to be with Ned, and she hoped she would have time to collect herself before the meeting. Besides, the weather report had predicted severe thunderstorms, and Paula hated the thought of being caught out in the unprotected fields during a bad wind. She definitely didn't want to go to the preserve.

The students waited anxiously for her reply. These two had begun the year with the misconception that her course in environmental science would be a rehash of Saturday morning cartoons about recycling. When they had learned that she expected them to understand the basics of complexity theory and the relationship between physics, chemistry, and biology as well as the details about various ecosystems, both of them had attempted to transfer to art appreciation. Unfortunately, that class had been so full that the guidance counselor denied the request. To Paula's delight, John and Connie had made the best of the situation and decided to learn something about earth science. They struggled to keep up with the students who had taken chemistry, but they did seem to be learning a good deal. The teacher in her won out over her misgivings.

"All right. I need to go home and change first, but I can meet you there in about an hour." She looked at Connie's delicate pastel sandals. "Do you have boots? It's likely to be pretty wet out there."

"We'll stop and change, too," Connie assured her. "Thanks a lot, Ms. Rosewood!"

They tore down the stairs, rushing to satisfy the one extra-credit project that required more diligence and labor than intimate understanding. Paula smiled and continued down the steps.

As she entered her apartment, her phone rang. Parker's voice greeted her with his usual exuberance. "Can you believe this guy? He is incredible!"

"Sorry, Parker." She carried the phone in the crook of her neck as she pulled on her boots. "I haven't talked with him. What's the news?"

"He heard about some new membranes, and by installing them at our source point from the soaking tanks, we may increase our product yield by about three percent. They weren't even developed for ethanol production. Some Japanese company developed them for wastewater treatment, and Ned thought they might help us with our xylose-glucose recovery. It could be a substantial breakthrough. It will certainly allow me to make an adequate profit to operate!"

"You're right. He's incredible." Paula steeled herself against the disappointment that Ned hadn't called her with the news. After all, she had not intended to start up the relationship again.

"Well, I had to let you know about this, but I guess our meeting is off for tonight. Ned said he had to check out some property out in the county."

Paula debated whether to feel relieved or defeated and finally decided to feel nothing. Instead she went in search of her aspiring naturalists. She found them leaning against the fender of a Volvo station wagon as she braked her Cavalier beside them. The lot of a teacher is not always a happy one, she thought, shoving down her envy.

"Okay, you two, here's the scoop. This early in the season, all we need to do is make certain that the birdhouses are clean." She demonstrated her "look-knock-open" routine and explained that the birds had not yet started this season's nesting. "Anything you find will be a leftover from last year, or a dummy nest from this year's hopeful male wrens. As warm as the weather has been this season, you may find some wasps building nests and there might be a snake looking for something, but mostly I think you'll just have trash to clean out." She handed them each a pair of gloves and sent them off in the direction opposite the one she took.

As she worked her way around the trail, Paula could almost hear Hector barking and Ned calling him back as he had that first day they met. She looked across the preserve land and into the next field where the plant construction continued to progress. With Parker's approval and the help of the beginning shop class at school, Paula had managed to put up twenty bluebird houses on a path in that field. She wondered if any of her other students would volunteer to do clean-up duty for extra credit, or if John and Connie would try to convince her to bend her rule to allow them to do the same project twice.

She opened a box, the wren's nest within filling the square with its neat, rough twigs. No feathers, no soft grass, no eggs. Probably, the female had never even seen this nest. She probably hadn't even decided which male she liked the best. Her house was about to be torn down before she even had a chance. Paula thought about the tiny wren. Little

Jenny Wren. An intruder species. An interloper. As much as she might be loved and wanted in a garden, she was persona non grata on the bluebird trail. These houses belonged to the threatened and beautiful bluebird and tree swallow, not to the ordinary, rugged wren.

Totally unnoticed by her, Paula's cheeks grew wet as tears slid past her eyelashes and down her cheeks. *Poor little wren,* she thought, *I don't want to destroy your husband's gift to you. Who says you're the intruder species? Why can't you have a home like anyone else? Why shouldn't you be allowed in this space just because it was originally intended for someone else? Why should you be denied just because you aren't the first choice?* Her arguments had nothing to do with the birds and everything to do with herself. She stood paralyzed, her fingers touching the dummy nest, but not removing it from the box.

"Hey! Are you some kid vandalizing the bird nests?" The whispered words floated to her so softly, she wondered at first if she had actually heard them or only fantasized them.

"No short-people jokes!" She spoke sharply to cover her tears, but he must have heard them anyway.

"What's wrong? Has something happened?" He reached around her, placed his hands gently on her shoulders, and slowly spun her to face him. "Paula. What is it?" He reached into his pocket and brought out a handkerchief, which he used to dry her tears and then handed to her.

"It's nothing." She laughed a little. "It's the birds. I'm crying about the birds. Isn't that silly of me? . . . it's not ironed."

"What? I don't understand."

"It's not ironed. Why didn't you iron it?"

"The bird? What are you talking about?"

Paula fought with herself. She could explain her meaning. She would explain her meaning, just as soon as he took his hands off her shoulders so she could concentrate again. His fingers pressed into the muscles of her arms, drawing her closer to him, and his eyes stared deeply into hers.

"What?" She tried to recover the thread of their conversation, but only one word came to her mind: Ned. "Ned."

He moved his face down toward hers, never releasing her eyes from their imprisonment by his own. "Paula."

"Hey, Ms. Rosewood! Ms. Rosewood! We cleaned all the birdhouses and then we found another one down in the woods! Oops! Sorry!" John came screeching to a halt as he rounded the curve in the trail and spied Paula and Ned. His face turned the shade of a sun-ripened tomato as Paula and Ned quickly stepped apart. "Uh, I, uh. Gee. I mean, do you want us to clean out that other box—the one down in the woods?"

Ignoring Ned's sparkling eyes and mischievous grin, Paula took another step away from him and replied. "This is Mr. Andersen, John. He cleans up other people's messes."

Ned barked with laughter, causing John to turn even redder with confusion. "Sometimes I even clean up my own messes."

Paula continued, "Don't pay any attention to him, John. The box in the woods is much larger than these, isn't it?"

"Yes ma'am. And it's nailed to a tree."

"It's for wood ducks. You can check it and clean it, but we probably won't have to worry about it again. The house wrens don't like such large houses."

"Their needs are simple, but they fight like the devil to get those needs met," Ned added, still grinning at Paula.

"Okay," answered John, retreating as quickly as possible back into the woods.

Ned turned back to Paula, taking a step toward her even as she backed up. "Paula?" He spoke as if daring her to continue to move.

This wasn't how she had expected things to go between them. She had expected a final, firm closure of their relationship, a civilized conversation held in a public restaurant to minimize the likelihood that she would break down. They had separated, she had thought, and now it was time to end all of the hurts. So why did he continue to advance toward her even as she retreated?

Talk, she thought. They had always been able to keep a wall of words between them like a bundling board to protect their virtue. "So why didn't you iron your handkerchief, Ned?" She asked as she trotted down the path towards the woods and the safety of her students' presence.

"Paula, do you really want to talk about my greatly deteriorated housekeeping habits? Is that what's really on your mind?" He seemed to be having no difficulty keeping up with her, and she was unexpectedly becoming breathless. She must be more out of shape than she thought.

"Yes!" she insisted. "I've never seen you with an unironed anything before! Have you been ill again? Did something happen to you out in the desert?"

"Why are you in such a hurry, Paula?" She was practically running now and increasing her speed at every step. "No. I have not been ill again. Yes. Something happened to me in the desert."

Abruptly she slowed her pace to a walk. "What happened to you? Were you hurt?"

He stopped walking, knowing that he had her attention completely now, and that she would not continue to try to run away. As soon as she realized he had fallen behind, she returned to him on the trail. "Were you? Were you hurt?"

"No. Not exactly." He leaned closer, and she backed away again, confused by this aggressive flavor in his body language.

"What, then? I thought we were going to have dinner tonight and talk things over."

Ned reached for her right hand and captured it in his left before she could jerk it away. "Come with me, Paula. I have something to show you."

John and Connie's laughter sounded through the trees, at Connie's being startled by a tiny spring peeper jumping out of her way. They splashed through the swamp to reach the wood duck house.

"I can't leave here until we're finished. If I leave those two babes alone in the woods, I will be committing a terrible act of negligence."

"Come on, Paula. They're old enough to look out for themselves."

"I'm not worried about them; I'm worried about the woods!" She pulled her hand away and rounded the curve of the trail that headed into the wooded swamp area, softly calling to the two students to keep the noise down. When she turned to see if Ned had followed, she nearly collided with him, so closely did he tread on her heels.

"I'm not letting you get away from me until I have shown you what I want to show you," he insisted, grabbing her hand again.

"All right," she capitulated. "We're almost finished here, anyway."

John and Connie slogged through the muddy water, quite proud of themselves for their willingness to sacrifice cleanliness for environmental health. "We did it, Ms. Rosewood. Actually it wasn't terribly messy, but it seemed like it might have been the remains of an old nest from last year."

"That's right." She nodded. "Now we won't have to clean that box when the water is even higher. All right, you two. Go home and write two pages about the bluebird trail and why we did what we did out here. I expect you to include some of the theoretical information we've learned in class about the interrelationships between species. That should give both of you enough extra credit to get you through most of the quarter."

With thanks and a little shoving of each other, the two teenagers dripped their way back to their car while Paula and Ned sauntered slowly around the rest of the trail. Ned did not release Paula's hand, even while she instructed her students, and she had become uncomfortably aware that he had begun stroking her with his thumb. He held her right hand with his left, and as her perceptions centered on his touch, she became aware that he was not wearing his wedding ring. She stopped walking, taking his hand in both of hers.

"Ned?" She traced the tender, sunburned skin around his third finger and looked up at him questioning the missing jewelry.

With his right hand he reached out and traced his index finger across her lips. "Not yet. Come with me first."

She wanted to ask where and why. She wanted to

yell at him to explain this change. Instead she said simply, "Yes. I'll come."

They returned to their cars; John and Connie were long gone from the lot, and Ned opened the passenger door of his car for Paula to enter. As he left the preserve he turned toward Centerville, rather than toward Preston, and Paula started to question again but held her tongue.

"Paula, tell me about the birds."

"What?" She once again felt disoriented by his conversation.

"Tell me about the wrens. Why did the wren's nest make you cry."

She heaved a deep sigh, as if she hadn't the energy to delve once again into the pain the nest had caused her. Ned took his right hand off the steering wheel and held it out to her. This time Paula reached for him and stroked his palm with that soothing circular motion he had once used on her.

"Do you know what wrens do during nesting season?" she asked.

"No. Tell me."

"Each year the male checks out the nesting sites for the female. He builds nests in every site he can find. One male can build up to six dummy nests in an afternoon if he can find enough good locations. He will fill up the boxes with dummies that the female will never use. Sometimes he will destroy the other birds' eggs and build on top of their nests, just to protect his territory and impress his female. That's the reason the wrens are so dangerous to the bluebirds and tree swallows.

"Wrens are wonderful little birds to have around, but on the bluebird trail they are interlopers. A lot of times, the volunteers become so attached to the bluebirds that they want to clear out a legitimate wren's nest, one that the female has selected and prepared for her eggs. Of course, that's illegal, and we explain that as a native species, the wren must also be protected; but the attitude is that the bluebird is the only bird that has the right to live on the bluebird trail.''

Ned wrapped his fingers around Paula's thumb, trapping it in his hand. "You were sympathizing with the wren."

"Yes."

"I understand."

She sighed again. "I know. You always do."

Ned slowed the car and turned up a graveled drive that wound up a small, wooded hill. Before he reached the top, the gravel petered out and he continued driving on a dirt track. Near the summit, the land had been cleared in one direction, and Paula looked out over the slightly rolling countryside. The roofs of Centerville presented an uneven pattern off to her right, and to the left of the town, the afternoon shadows deepened the blue of the Centerville reservoir.

"How beautiful this is!" she exclaimed to Ned as she climbed out of the car. "Is this what you wanted to show me?"

Instead of answering, he asked another question. "How do the wrens decide which nest to use?"

Paula held very still as he approached her. "The male shows his nests to the female and she selects one by beginning to add her own touches to it. She adds feathers and grass to make it soft and ready for the eggs."

Ned took both of her hands in his and looked around at the land below them. "I think that the only trouble with wrens is that they need their own houses. They aren't like Sarah's bald eagles that must return to the same place for ever and ever. Wrens know how to adapt, how to find new homes where they can be just as happy as they were before. Maybe even happier.''

Paula nodded. "Maybe.''

"Paula, I don't have six different nesting sites to show you, only this one. But if you don't like it, I could very easily keep looking. I think the important thing is that we build our nest together. That way it will always be our own.''

He lifted one hand to tilt her chin up toward his face and lowered his head toward hers, but she placed her fingers on his lips before he could kiss her.

"Are you sure, Ned? Are you really sure this time?''

He kissed the fingers she held to his mouth and then pulled away her hand. "As sure as I have ever been about anything in my life.'' Then with a sardonic smile, he changed that. "No. I am more sure than I have ever been about anything in my life. I know more than I did at twenty. I certainly know myself better than I did at thirty. And I know you. I am sure.''

Once again he bent to kiss her, and once again she stopped him. Ned sighed and lifted his eyebrows in question.

"What happened in the desert?'' She wanted to know; she needed to know if she was going to trust this change in him.

They sat on a small outcropping of rock, looking over the greening fields surrounding Centerville, and he told her about his pilgrimage up the desert mountain. "I finally faced what I haven't been able to face from the beginning of Annie's illness. There are some things I have no control over, and her death

was one of those things. It's still amazing to me that
I managed to be in denial for all those years without
even knowing it.''

''I suppose that's what denial is . . . not knowing
it.'' She put her hand on his in comfort.

''Sean tried to tell me, that day last fall. I guess
he saw through all my talk about coping and dealing
with things. I just didn't want to listen to him.''

Paula gazed across the fields, the setting sun cast-
ing long shadows softened by the beginning of an
evening haze. ''I think you had to get here by yourself, Ned. Sean couldn't help you and neither could
I. You had to want to face the truth yourself.''

''But you did help me, Paula.'' He touched her
hair softly as he spoke. ''You gave me something to
make life worthwhile again. I had a reason for facing
the truth because not facing it kept me from you.''
He placed his hands on her cheeks and once more
pulled her toward himself to kiss her, but Paula still
resisted.

''Where is your ring?''

He shook his head in frustration. ''You're mer-
ciless! I left it in the desert. I buried it, actually.''
He blushed a little as he remembered the intensely
personal act. ''I sort of had a ceremony. I said good-
bye to Annie. And I left the ring there where I think
it's pretty unlikely to be disturbed for a long, long
time.'' He grabbed Paula by the arms and held them
to her sides. ''Now if you don't want me to kiss
you, I want to know why.''

Totally unexpected tears sprang to Paula's eyes,
and she trembled beneath his hands.

''Paula! Oh, Paula, what's wrong?'' Ned rapidly
sank into a pit of despair as he searched her face for
an explanation of her resistance to him, but through
her tears Paula had begun to smile.

"Oh, you fool. I don't want you to kiss me because I'm not sure I can handle such happiness."

The sun set with a rapidity that would have startled them if either had bothered to notice, and the cooling evening air would have chilled them if they had not held each other so closely that they created their own warmth. At last no more words blanketed their tenderness, no more work exhausted their energy, no more ghosts haunted their souls. They kissed long and sweetly, only separating at last so they could begin planning their nest.

When Paula and Ned moved into their new home following their return from their October honeymoon, they held a housewarming party for their many friends. Paula's fellow teachers had already given the gift of their time by helping with the move, but Barbara brought an additional gift.

"Do you remember what I said to you a year ago about 'a bird in the hand?' " she asked Paula.

"I have begun to think of my entire life as an endless list of clichés!" moaned Paula. "As I recall, I didn't want to listen to you, and as it turned out, I was right."

"You were. Well, this gift is an acknowledgment of your being right," she said as she pulled a framed needlepoint design from a bag. "Hang this in a place that will remind you."

The brightly colored work depicted bluebirds, swallows, cardinals, and finches surrounding a bush on which perched two tiny wrens. Below the picture were the words:

A bird in the bush
Usually has a friend in there with him.